SEVEN YEAR SWITCH

Seven Year Switch

Claire Cook

voice

Hyperion · New York

Library of Congress Cataloging-in-Publication Data

Cook, Claire
    Seven year switch / Claire Cook.
        p.   cm.
    ISBN 978-1-4013-4116-9
    1. Single mothers—Fiction.   2. Self-realization in women—Fiction.
    3. Domestic fiction.   I. Title.
    PS3553.O55317S48   2010
    813'.54—dc22

                                                    2009045959

Hyperion books are available for special promotions and premiums. For details contact the HarperCollins Special Markets Department in the New York office at 212-207-7528, fax 212-207-7222, or email spsales@harpercollins.com.

FIRST EDITION

10 9 8 7 6 5 4 3 2 1

THIS LABEL APPLIES TO TEXT STOCK

TO OLD FRIENDS,

NEW FRIENDS,

FACEBOOK FRIENDS

ACKNOWLEDGMENTS

First and foremost, a zillion thanks to you, my readers. Whenever you take time out of your busy lives to read one of my novels, send it to your sister on her birthday, tell a friend you liked it (and make her buy her own copy!) you breathe life into my next book. On this most basic, sustaining level, without you I wouldn't be having the best midlife career switch ever, and I appreciate your support, especially in this crazy world and tough economy, more than I can say.

But wait, there's more. I think reader response is so important that it sometimes feels as if I don't completely know what I've written until you tell me what you've read. Your messages and reviews lift me up and keep me on track. You get it, you really get it! Thank you.

Many, many thanks to my fabulous bookseller, librarian, journalist, and blogger friends and supporters—I appreciate you truly, madly, deeply.

While I was writing this novel, a small group of women generously shared buried pieces of their past with me. Your stories helped me find the heart of this book, and I'm so thankful for them. And, as promised, your secrets are my secrets!

Thank you to the kind people of San José and Tamarindo for help along the way, as well as to Charlotte Phinney, Maria Sanchez, and Anna Holmes. Thanks to Ken Harvey for another caring, insightful read.

Heartfelt thanks to Tammy Orrell for never missing one of my book events within a hundred miles' drive. It was an honor to be your favorite author. Rest in peace, Tammy, and thank you, Jessica, for letting me know.

I thank my lucky stars for the wonderful women (and a few good men) at Hyperion/Voice. When you shine your collective brilliance on my books, you light up my world. Thanks for focusing so much attention on this grateful woman's voice. Thanks, thanks, and more thanks to my wonderful editor, Brenda Copeland, her terrific assistant, Kate Griffin, and to the rest of the talented Hyperionites: Ellen Archer, Barbara Jones, Mindy Stockfield, Sarah Rucker, Marie Coolman, Allison McGeehon, Katherine Tasheff, Maha Khalil, Mike Rotondo, Joan Lee, Claire McKean, Laura Klynstra, Lindsay Mergens, Shelley Perron, Shubhani Sarkar, and Karen Minster. Thank you to the HarperCollins sales force for your support—with an extra shout-out to Donna Waitkus and a special thanks to Andrea Rosen and her team for inspiring a scene in this book at our meeting!

Lisa Bankoff's support is always above and beyond, and I'm more thankful with each and every book. A huge thank you to ICM's unflappable agent-to-be Elizabeth Perrella, to the wonderful Josie Freedman, and to magazine maven Alison Schwartz. Many thanks to Helen Manders and Curtis Brown Group for their foreign rights enthusiasm.

Mega thanks and much love to Jake, Kaden, and Garet for stepping up whenever I need it. You're simply the best.

"It is never too late to be what you might have been."

GEORGE ELIOT

SEVEN YEAR SWITCH

I SAILED INTO THE COMMUNITY CENTER JUST IN TIME TO take my Lunch Around the World class to China. I hated to be late, but my daughter, Anastasia, had forgotten part of her school project.

"Oh, honey," I'd said when she called from the school office. "Can't it wait till tomorrow? I'm just leaving for work." I tried not to wallow in it, but sometimes the logistics of being a single mom were pretty exhausting.

"Mom," she whispered, "it's a diorama of a cow's habitat, and I forgot the *cow*."

I remembered seeing the small plastic cow grazing next to Anastasia's cereal bowl at breakfast, but how it had meandered into the dishwasher was anyone's guess. I gave it a quick rinse under the faucet and let it air-dry on the ride to school. From there I hightailed it to the community center.

Though it wasn't the most challenging part of my work week, this Monday noon-to-two-o'clock class got me home before my daughter, which in the dictionary of my life made it the best kind of gig. Sometimes I even had time for a cup of tea before her school bus came rolling down the street. Who knew a cup of tea could be the most decadent part of your day.

I plopped my supplies on the kitchen counter and jumped right in. "In Chinese cooking, it's important to balance colors as well as contrasts in tastes and textures."

"Take a deep breath, honey," one of my favorite students said. Her name was Ethel, and she had bright orange lips and *I Love Lucy* hair. "We're not going anywhere."

A man with white hair and matching eyebrows started singing "On a Slow Boat to China." A couple of the women giggled. I took that deep breath.

"*Yum cha* is one of the best ways to experience this," I continued. "Literally, *yum cha* means 'drinking tea,' but it actually encompasses both the tea drinking and the eating of dim sum, a wide range of light dishes served in small portions."

"Yum-yum," a man named Tom said. His thick glasses were smudged with fingerprints, and he was wearing a T-shirt that said TUNE IN TOMORROW FOR A DIFFERENT SHIRT.

"Let's hope," I said. "In any case, *dim sum* has many translations: 'small eats,' of course, but also 'heart's delight,' 'to touch your heart,' and even 'small piece of heart.' I've often wondered if Janis Joplin decided to sing the song she made famous after a dim sum experience."

Last night when I was planning my lesson, this had seemed like a brilliant and totally original cross-cultural connection, but everybody just nodded politely.

We made dumplings and pot stickers and mini spring rolls, and then we moved on to fortune cookies. Custard tarts or even mango pudding would have been more culturally accurate, but fortune cookies were always a crowd-pleaser. I explained that the crispy, sage-laced cookies had actually been invented in San Francisco, and tried to justify my choice by adding that the original inspiration for fortune cookies possibly dated back to the thirteenth century, when Chinese soldiers slipped rice paper messages into mooncakes to help coordinate their defense against Mongolian invaders.

Last night Anastasia had helped me cut small strips of white paper to write the fortunes on. And because the cookies had to be wrapped around the paper as soon as they came out of the oven, while they were still pliable, I'd bought packages of white cotton gloves at CVS and handed out one to each person. The single gloves kept the students' hands from burning and were less awkward than using pot holders.

They also made the class look like aging Michael Jackson impersonators. A couple of the women started to sing "Beat It" while they stirred the batter, and then everybody else joined in. There wasn't a decent singer in the group, but some of them could still remember how to moonwalk.

After we finished packing up some to take home, we'd each placed one of our cookies in a big bamboo salad bowl. There'd been more giggling as we passed the bowl around the long, wobbly wooden table and took turns choosing a cookie and reading the fortune, written by an anonymous classmate, out loud.

" 'The time is right to make new friends.' "

" 'A great adventure is in your near future.' "

" 'A tall dark-haired man will come into your life.' "

" 'You will step on the soil of many countries, so don't forget to pack clean socks.' "

" 'The one you love is closer than you think,' " Ethel read. Her black velour sweat suit was dusted with flour.

"Oo-ooh," the two friends taking the class with her said. One of them elbowed her.

The fortune cookies were a hit. So what if my students seemed more interested in the food than in its cultural origins. I wondered if they'd still have signed up if I'd shortened the name of the class from Lunch Around the World to just plain Lunch. My class had been growing all session, and not a single person had asked for a refund. In this economy, everybody was cutting everything, and even community center classes weren't immune. The best way to stay off the chopping block was to keep your classes full and your students happy.

I reached over and picked up the final fortune cookie, then looked at my watch. "Oops," I said. "Looks like we're out of time." I stood and smiled at the group. "Okay, everybody, that's it for today." I nodded at the take-out cartons I'd talked the guy at the Imperial Dragon into donating to the cause. "Don't forget your cookies, and remember, next week we'll be lunching in Mexico." I took care to pronounce it *Mehico*.

"Tacos?" T-shirt Tom asked.

"You'll have to wait and see-eee," I said, mostly because I hadn't begun to think about next week. Surviving this one was enough of a challenge.

"Not even a hint?" a woman named Donna said.

I shook my head and smiled some more.

They took their time saying thanks and see you next week as they grabbed their take-out boxes by the metal handles and headed out the door. A few even offered to help me pack up, but I said I was all set. It was faster to do it myself.

As I gave the counters a final scrub, I reviewed the day's class in my head. Overall, I thought it had gone well, but I still didn't understand why the Janis Joplin reference had fallen flat.

I put the sponge down, picked up a wooden spoon, and got ready to belt out "Piece of My Heart."

When I opened my mouth, a chill danced the full length of my spine. I looked up. A man was standing just outside the doorway. He had dark, wavy hair cascading almost to his shoulders and pale, freckled skin. He was tall and a little too thin. His long fingers gripped the doorframe, as if a strong wind might blow him back down the hallway.

He was wearing faded jeans and the deep green embroidered Guatemalan shirt I'd given my husband just before he abandoned us seven years ago.

No. Way.

I'd dreamed this scene a thousand times, played it out hundreds of different ways.

I'd kissed him and killed him over and over and over again, violently and passionately, and at every emotional stop in between.

"Jill?" he said.

My mouth didn't seem to be working. *That's my name, don't wear it out* popped into my head randomly, as if to prove my brain wasn't firing on all cylinders either.

"Can I talk to you for a minute?" he said.

My heart leaped into action and my hands began to shake, but other than that, I couldn't feel a thing. I remembered reading that in a fight-or-flight reaction, deep thought shuts down and more primitive responses take over.

I picked up the bowl. I gulped down some air. I measured the distance between us. I tried to imagine my feet propelling me past him—out of the building, into my car, safely back home. Flight was winning by a landslide.

"No," I said. "Actually, you can't."

He followed me out to my car, keeping a safe distance. I clicked the lock and balanced the bowl on my left hip while I opened the door of my battered old Toyota.

"How is she?" he asked. "How's Asia?"

"Her *name* is Anastasia," I said.

But the damage had been done. In one nickname, four letters, he'd brought it all back. We'd spent much of my pregnancy tracing our family trees online, looking for the perfect name for our daughter-to-be. In a sea of Sarahs and Claras and Helens, Anastasia jumped right out, a long-forgotten relative on Seth's side of the family. Since we didn't have any details, we made up our own. Our daughter would be Anastasia, the lost princess of

Russia. Sometimes she'd have escaped the revolution only to be frozen to wait for the perfect parents to be born. Other times she came to us via simple reincarnation. We'd curled up on our shabby couch in front of our hand-me-down TV and watched the animated *Anastasia* over and over again, until we could do most of the voice-overs right along with Meg Ryan and John Cusack.

When she was born, Anastasia brought her own twist to the story. From a combined ethnic pool swimming with ancestors from Ireland, England, Scotland, Italy, and Portugal, she'd somehow inherited the most amazing silky straight dark hair and exotic almond-shaped eyes. We nicknamed her Asia, a continent we loved, the place we'd met.

I closed my eyes. "She's ten," I said. "She's fine. I'm fine. Leave us alone, Seth. Just leave us the fuck alone."

By the time I opened my eyes, he was already walking away.

It wasn't until I went to put my hands on the steering wheel that I realized I was still holding my fortune cookie. It had shattered into pieces, and the thin strip of paper inside had morphed into a crumb-and-sweat-covered ball. I peeled it off my palm.

Something you lost will soon show up.

"Thanks for the warning," I said.

2

"GREAT GIRLFRIEND GETAWAYS," I SAID INTO MY HEAD-phone as Anastasia reached for another pot sticker with her chopsticks. "Feisty and fabulous man-free escapes both close to home and all over the world. When was the last time you got together with *your* girlfriends?"

"Hello?" a female voice said into my ear. "Is this a real person?"

That was probably a question to be pondered, but I gave her the short answer. "Yes," I said. "This is Jill, one of GGG's cultural consultants, available twenty-four/seven to help you plan the girlfriend getaway of your dreams. How can I help you?"

"Okay, well, my friends and I are thinking about your trip to the Dominican, but somebody I work with said she went to an all-inclusive there and saw an actual rat in her room, and I don't do rats. Can you guarantee me a rat-free room? In writing?"

I wasn't sure I could guarantee her a rat-free room in New York, but why get into it. Anastasia picked up her plate and started sliding her chair back. I narrowed my eyes and gave her a mom glare.

"Well," I said, "if you want to keep the pests at bay, we've also got a trip to Italy coming up. It includes one full day on Beach 134, aka the Pink Beach, the official no-men-allowed beach on the Adriatic coast."

I waited for a laugh. Nothing. Anastasia was tiptoeing across the kitchen. I stamped my foot. She kept walking.

"The signs alone will make your photo album," I said. "They've got this one huge sign with an Italian version of the Marlboro man in an old-fashioned bathing suit getting ready to hit on somebody, and he's got a great big diagonal line drawn through him."

Of course, I'd never actually seen this sign, but I'd added the photo to our brochure and also uploaded it to the Web site.

"I don't know," the woman said. "I bet the guys still pinch you as soon as you get off the beach. And doesn't Italy have rats, too?"

I pinched off a little piece of pork dumpling and popped it into my mouth.

I covered the phone and swallowed quickly. "Orlando's nice this time of year," I finally said.

"I don't know. We really wanted to absorb another culture."

I rolled my eyes and reached for another pinch of pork. "You can always go to Epcot."

"Good point. Okay, so do you recommend the Epcot-only International Pajama Party or the Careening-thru-Kissimmee Multi-Theme Park Girlfriend Adventure?"

In so many ways, this job had saved my life, and I knew how lucky I was to have it. Joni Robertson, Great Girlfriend Getaways' owner, paid me enough of a salary to almost make ends meet, as well as about half of Anastasia's and my health insurance. She'd also given me a computer to replace my dinosaur when she upgraded her office equipment, and even paid half my cell phone bill so I had somewhere to forward the GGG calls. But the best thing was that she let me do most of my work from home and gave me enough flexibility to pick up jobs on the side.

I couldn't have made it without Joni. If I were in charge of the world, I'd get rid of all the Oscars and the Grammys and just give awards to women who helped other women.

Sure, I'd imagined that by this point in my life, I'd be a little further along in my career as a cultural consultant. A dual major in international government and sociocultural anthropology, I'd envisioned myself as a pioneer in the emerging field of cross-cultural coaching. After getting my feet wet in the corporate world, where I'd be brilliantly successful at training executives to become more effective global communicators, I'd build my own international consulting business. I pictured myself jetting around, preparing foreign service families before they headed off to their posts, helping to greenwash small countries trying to step up their ecotourism trade, counseling rising politicians who thought they could see Russia from their backyards.

And then life got in the way.

Here's the thing that really pisses me off when I listen to those women on TV with their big salaries, or their trust funds, or their great family support. They're up on their high horses in their rarefied worlds telling the rest of us women we shouldn't jump off the career track or we'll never get back on. We should just follow our dreams, go after what we want, come hell or high water.

But what if scrambling to pay the bills takes every minute of your day, every ounce of your creativity? What if you can't afford an au pair? What if you can't even afford an ordinary babysitter? And even if you could, which you can't, what if your three-year-old is so afraid that you're going to leave her, too, that she spends most of an entire year holding on to your leg, and somedays, just to do the vacuuming, you have to drag her around the room with you?

Eventually I got Rat Girl off the phone. I popped the rest of the dumpling into my mouth, took half a second to appreciate the warm burst of ginger and green onion, and pushed back my own chair.

I poked my head into the living room. "You've got until three to turn that TV off and get back to the dinner table."

Anastasia ignored me.

"One," I said.

She ignored me some more.

"Two," I said.

"Mom," she said. "It's almost over."

"Anabanana . . . ," I said.

She jumped up. "*Don't* call me that. It's a baby name."

My daughter, all elbows and knees in purple leggings and a long striped T-shirt dress, flounced past me with her empty plate. She adjusted her shiny pink headband with one hand as she came in for a landing at the kitchen table. I tried hard to give her the firm, consistent limits all kids need, but the truth was I loved her little acts of rebellion. I read them as signs of progress, evidence that she had not only survived, but was finally starting to thrive. She had friends at school. Her grades were good. She loved to read.

The last thing either of us needed was for Seth to come back into our lives and screw them all up again.

MY PHONE SHIFT TONIGHT was four to midnight. After Anastasia was in bed, I made myself a cup of Earl Grey tea so I could stay awake. Some nights the phone rang like crazy, and I'd talk nonstop about group rates and trip insurance and the relative merits of Provence versus Paris while I washed dishes or folded the laundry. I'd gotten so used to going about my business while I talked into my headphone that once I even flushed the toilet while I was talking to some woman about our Galapagos Islands cruise.

"What was *that*?" she'd asked.

"Just a waterfall," I'd replied. "The Iguazu? On the Brazil-Argentina border?"

"Ooh," she said. "Can you send me some info on that trip, too?"

Tonight was quiet. Eerily quiet. Twice I got up and walked over to the living room window that looked out over the street. I pulled back the curtain just enough to peek out without being seen. As hard as I tried, I couldn't detect a trace of Seth. But whether he was actually out there after all, or simply hovering on the outskirts of our lives, I could feel him.

Just as the big old predigital clock on the living room wall was reaching its long pointy arm up to midnight, I pulled off my headphone and pushed myself away from the couch.

I took my time heading to my bedroom. There was no rush: my life had turned back into a pumpkin a long, long time ago.

3

ANASTASIA HAD NIXED THE KISS AT THE BUS STOP AROUND this time last year. We said our good-byes inside the house now, and then I sat on the front steps, looking up and down the street for potential kidnappers and pedophiles while she waited with the other kids and pretended I wasn't there.

"Hi there," Cynthia from next door said as she came over to join me. For a minute, it looked like she might even sit down beside me on the cement steps. Whether it was the potential damage to her tennis skirt or her manicure that stopped her, I might never know. She rested one hand on the metal railing instead.

"Hey," I said. I kept my eyes on Anastasia. I'd never admit it to anyone, but even though she was in fourth grade now, I still got a tiny bit choked up every time the bus pulled away.

Cynthia lifted her hand off the railing and examined it.

"It's called rust," I said.

"Don't *we* have a big chip on our shoulder this morning," she said. "God, you never seem to amaze me."

While I puzzled over her morning malaprop, Cynthia grabbed a chunk of impeccably foiled hair with her rust-free hand, stretched it diagonally across her forehead, and held it there, as if she were teaching it how to stay. "So, how about lunch at that new sushi place on Maple?" she finally asked.

I tried to like Cynthia, I really did. She reminded me of that old *don't hate me because I'm beautiful* commercial, and she drove me almost as crazy. It was hard not to hate someone, at least a little, when they oozed entitlement from every well-peeled and dermabraded pore, but I also kind of wanted to *be* Cynthia. Somehow I thought I'd do a better job of it.

Cynthia and her family buying the house next door last year had been a sign that the neighborhood was on its way up. Anastasia and I moved in three years earlier with the help of a no-money-down, low-interest program for first-time buyers. Joni, my boss, had not only helped me find it, but also gave me some hand-me-down furniture and a paid day off to move. It was considered a "transitional" neighborhood then, though "sketchy" might have been more accurate.

But the neighborhood had gone from transitional to trendy, and now people like Cynthia couldn't wait to get their hands on the funky little summer cottages, so they could double or triple the square footage and deck them out into full-blown year-round housing extravaganzas. With every year that passed, my mostly untouched house looked smaller in comparison but also grew a lot more valuable. Maybe eventually my neighbors would pool their pocket change and plop an addition on mine, too, just to keep me up with the Joneses.

The bus pulled up in front of my house. I stood up. Anastasia held on to the front straps of her pink backpack as she climbed aboard with the other kids. She took a seat where I could see her and leaned back against her backpack like a pillow. I waved. She lifted one hand casually, maybe a wave, maybe not, then started fine-tuning her headband.

After the bus had pulled away, I turned to Cynthia. "Sorry," I said, "but I can't. I've got a client today."

Cynthia reached up with both hands to check on her chunky gold earrings. "All work and no play-ay," she sang, "make Jill a dull gull."

"Thanks," I said. I thought about adding a little seagull screech, but I wasn't sure I could pull it off.

Supposedly, Cynthia worked, too. She said she had her own interior decorating business, but I'd yet to see evidence of a client, interior or exterior, to back up the claim.

I took a step toward my door. "Yeah, well, have a tuna roll for me, okay?"

"Eat your own mercury. Hey, if I'm not back in time, can you grab my three off the bus and give them a quick snack?"

I looked at her. Cynthia was simply one of those women who always came out on top. If you carpooled with her, you somehow managed to drive twice as often as she did. If you watched each other's kids, she got one and you got three. There was nothing to be done about it. It was just the way of the world. And I needed her for backup.

"Yeah, sure," I said. "Not a problem."

I WAS MEETING my new client at Starbucks. Of all the cultures in all the world, wouldn't you know he'd want to talk about Japan. But I couldn't afford to ruminate about brutal poetic irony when bills needed to be paid, so I had no choice but to take him on.

He'd gotten my name from an ad I'd placed on Craigslist, so he could easily turn out to be a nutcase. Starbucks was safe, private enough, and since he'd agreed right away to the insane hourly consulting rate I'd thrown out to leave room for negotiation, I could even afford the coffee.

A guy was chaining his bike to the bike rack next to Starbucks when I got there. I hurried past him and reached for the heavy front door.

"Yo," he said. "You're not Jill, are you?"

I turned around and watched him slide a big rubber band off one nylon pant leg while I considered which was the bigger red flag that this guy couldn't afford me, the *yo* or the bicycle.

"I am indeed," I said. I held out my hand. "Jill Murray. And you must be Bill Sanders."

"Billy," he said.

"Great," I said.

I'd half expected a high five or a knuckle tap, but at least he shook hands like a grown-up. He had good eye contact, too. His crinkly brown eyes had a bit of a raccoon quality, as if he spent a lot of time outside wearing sunglasses. He was probably about my age, though he seemed younger. Or maybe I just felt older.

Starbucks was teeming with people. I wondered if the whole world was doing away with their offices and coming here instead.

"How about you snare us a table, and I'll grab the coffee. Cappuccino okay?"

Technically, I should pick up the tab. I'd order a small regular coffee and hope he did, too.

I imagined gazing into the foam of a frothy, overpriced cappuccino. "Thanks," I said.

He handed me his bicycle helmet. I hovered near the tables, and as soon as two men stood up, I slid into a chair fast. I plopped the shiny green helmet in the middle of the table like a centerpiece.

When Billy Sanders eventually made his way over with my cappuccino, it turned out to be a venti. I said thanks and took a demure sip, since it seemed more dignified than yelling "score," but the truth was I couldn't wait for the day when I could just relax and buy whatever damn size overpriced coffee I wanted whenever I wanted to. "Okay," I said. I reached into my bag and pulled out an invoice. "Let's get the bookkeeping out of the way first, so we can get right to Japan."

He handed me a check that was already made out.

"Cool," slipped out of my mouth before I could stop it. I cleared my throat. "So, tell me what you need to know about Japanese culture, and why."

He took a moment to beat the bicycle helmet between us like a drum, ending with a single air cymbal crash. "The short version is that my family owns a business that makes bicycles."

I took another sip of foam-capped espresso heaven. "Must be nice," I said.

He shrugged. "It has its moments. Anyway, we have a core business with stable profits, and we're trying to balance some cuts we've made by investing in future growth."

He pushed a button on his cell phone and handed it to me.

I didn't know anything about bicycles, but the one on the screen was pretty amazing—sleek and shiny and futuristic. Most of the bike was an ultrametallic red, but its handlebars were painted so that they loomed above the front wheel like menacing eyes.

"Wow," I said. "It looks almost alive."

"Thanks," he said. "It's called the Akira. It's named after the Japanese anime from the '80s."

I squinted at the picture. "Of course it is."

"The design is a nod to the motorcycle the hero drives."

I nodded, as if I knew what he was talking about.

He looked over his shoulder for potential bicycle spies, then leaned toward me. "I had this idea that we'd test-market them in Tokyo. The bike rental market is already established there, but this would add a fresh, high-tech spin. Basically, we'd implant a microchip in each bike, and then people could locate the nearest bike with their smartphones. . . ."

I handed him back his iPhone. "And the bicycle would ride itself over to meet them?"

He smiled. "We're not quite there yet. But we'd sell inexpensive packages, and members would have access to hundreds of conveniently located, high-end Akira kiosks all over Tokyo. It'll be great advertising for bicycle sales, too, since the rental bikes will function like little billboards. And then, if the whole thing flies in Japan, we'll give it a shot in Boston. Car share companies like Zipcar are paving the way for us."

"Sounds like a great idea to me," I said. I took another sip of my cappuccino. "So what's the problem?"

He held both palms up toward the ceiling. "I can't get anybody to talk to me over there. I e-mailed some likely candidates, tried to set up some meetings. Nothing. So then I made some phone calls. I was like, hey, just say no if it doesn't sound good to you, but here's an idea that could make us both some money."

"There's your first problem," I said. "The Japanese don't like to say no. 'I'll consider it' means no. Sometimes even yes means no. You'll have to hire a go-between to set up the meetings, someone who speaks Japanese, has a good reputation, but also doesn't have a personal stake in the project. Make sure you wear a suit when you go. And bring gifts, but don't give them out until you see what they give you first, because it's important to match the level of your gifts to theirs. It can't be too extravagant a gift, because it might be considered a bribe, and make sure you don't open your gifts in front of them, and . . ."

Billy Sanders opened his raccoon eyes wide. "Seriously?" he said. "A suit-suit?"

4

I CERTAINLY DIDN'T NEED ANY MORE CAFFEINE, SO I skipped the tea and drank a glass of water when I got home. I had the noon-to-eight-o'clock shift, and the phone didn't waste any time ringing.

"Great Girlfriend Getaways," I said. "Feisty and fabulous man-free escapes—"

"Two minutes," Seth pleaded. "Just let me talk to you for two minutes. I've got a job, and I'll have a paycheck in a couple of weeks. I'm staying at my parents' for the time being. Listen, I want to see our daughter. I want to make things right."

I knew I should just hang up, but I couldn't seem to do it. "Make things right," I said. "Make. Things. Right." I could feel a heavy surf pounding in my ears.

I paced across the worn linoleum tiles on my kitchen floor. I started to open the back door, but changed my mind. There was nowhere to go.

"Seth, you cleaned out our bank account when you ran off. Do you know what that did to *our daughter* and me?"

He didn't say anything.

"Do you know what I found out, Seth? That they can't re-possess your car if you're in it. I *slept* in our car, Seth. For weeks. *Our daughter* slept in our car for weeks. In her Blues Clues sleeping bag with her entire collection of Beanie Babies. I told her we were fucking *camping*, Seth."

"I'm sorry," he said quietly.

I kept expecting my voice to catch, my eyes to tear up, but all I could feel was a cold, dry rage. I leaned against the kitchen counter and thumped my head into a cabinet.

"In a million years, you could never be sorry enough," I said calmly, as if I were stating a simple fact, like springtime is beautiful in the Netherlands.

"Why didn't you go to my parents?" He sounded like a little boy when he said it. It might have been *Why didn't you just ask Santa?*

"I did, Seth. It killed me, but I finally went to your parents. You know what they said? That they'd spent their whole lives cleaning up your messes, and they were finished. Your *messes*. And then on Anastasia's next birthday, they sent a Hallmark card that said 'Happy Birthday to a Fine Four-Year-Old' with a check inside for fifty fucking dollars. And I couldn't even afford to rip it up into a million pieces and send it back to them."

The pounding was back. Waves crashed in my ears like the soundtrack to *The Endless Summer*. I tried to slow my breathing so my head wouldn't explode. I always shocked myself a little when I heard the *f*-word come out of my mouth. It was crude. It was unsophisticated. But right now there weren't enough *fucks* in the world to express the depths of my rage.

"I'm sorry," Seth said softly.

"Seven years, Seth," I said. And then I hung up.

Seven years.

The Holo'o clan of the Sidama people in southern Ethiopia offers a sacrifice to their common ancestors every seven years. The Romans had seven deities. So did the Goths. Japanese folklore has the Seven Gods of Luck.

There are seven types of intelligence and seven habits for highly effective people. Hollywood has *Seventh Heaven* and

The Seven Year Itch. There's even a New Age notion that every seven years you shed your skin and become a completely new person, sort of a seven year switch.

There are seven seas and seven dwarfs, and if you break a mirror, superstition says you'll get seven years of bad luck. When asked to think of a number between one and ten, research shows that most people pick seven.

In twelfth-century Spain, Nachmanides formulated the kabbalistic concept that seven is the number of the natural world: seven days in the week, seven notes on the scale.

On a brisk spring day in twenty-first-century America, Jill Murray determined that a husband and father who stays away for seven years is unforgiveable.

EVEN THOUGH I WAS still tethered to my headphone, I herded all four kids over to Cynthia's house as soon as they got off the bus. No way was I going to let Cynthia's three trash my place while eating me out of house and home.

Cynthia always left a key under her welcome mat, not that a robber would ever think to look for it there. I lifted up the mat. Her youngest, Parker, stepped on my hand.

I screamed.

My cell rang.

Treasure, Cynthia's middle child, grabbed the key. Lexi, her oldest, grabbed it out of Treasure's hand. Treasure screamed. Anastasia adjusted her headband and watched like an anthropologist observing a fascinating new culture.

"Great Girlfriend Getaways," I said.

The kids disappeared into the house, leaving a trail of backpacks behind them like supersized bread crumbs.

Fortunately it turned out to be just a question about collecting on trip insurance, so all I had to do was recite the toll-free number of the insurance company from memory.

I was only a few steps behind them, but the kids had already grabbed snacks from the kiddie snack station, complete with miniature undercounter refrigerator, microwave, and snack drawers. Parker was heading for the mammoth flat-screen TV in the great room with a goji berry juice box and a bag of Spicy Nacho Doritos, and the three girls were carrying bottles of Perrier Pink Grapefruit and tubes of Kiwi Kick Go-Gurt to the three-computer kiddie work station in the large alcove off the great room, whatever that was called. The second greatest room?

I had to swallow a great big green gulp of envy every time I walked into this house. The excess was appalling, but also kind of seductive. I put my hand on a cool black granite counter and tried to guess which floor-to-ceiling cherry cabinet the adult refrigerator was hiding behind, since I could never remember until Cynthia opened it. Maybe it was part of the design strategy—make rich people thin by hiding the food.

My phone rang again. "Great Girlfriend Getaways," I said.

"Does she always talk into that thing?" Lexi asked from the middle computer.

Anastasia shrugged. Her shoulders stayed up around her ears. I knew that meant she was hoping against hope that her embarrassing mother would go away. This was a good thing. It was developmentally appropriate that she bond with her friends at my expense.

I walked down the long center hallway while I finished the rest of my spiel. "How can I help you?" I finally said.

"I'm in Spain?" a woman's voice said.

"Is that a question?" I asked.

"No, no, I know I'm in Spain. But I'm wondering if I should take the side trip to the Dalí museum in Figueres, or just stay here in Barcelona, since we went to the Picasso museum yesterday."

I opened a door off the hallway and stepped into a huge master bathroom: dual vanities, huge tumbled travertine tiles everywhere, a curved glass block wall that reminded me of an igloo, a toilet, a urinal. No, actually it was a bidet. Apparently someone forgot to tell Cynthia that bidets went out in the '80s.

I wasn't the kind of person who would normally snoop, but it was just a bathroom. I stepped inside and pulled the door closed behind me. A wisp of a pink negligee dangled from a heavy metal hook on the back of the door. I looked closer and saw that the tag was still on it. Maybe it was only a prop.

I walked across the room and peeked into the master bedroom, which had an unmade bed the size of a small continent, then closed the door again.

"Hello?"

"Oh, sorry," I said. "It's just that I'm not sure I'm following your question."

On a raised platform in the corner of the bathroom, a double, or even triple, garden tub looked out over the manicured backyard through a bay window. A remote rested on the ledge of the tub, and at one end, a flat-screen TV covered most of the wall.

"I mean, if I go all the way to Figueres, is it going to be same old, same old?"

You mean, are there going to be a lot of Picassos in the Dalí museum? I wanted to say, but I restrained myself. Surely this woman couldn't think if she'd been to one art museum, she'd been to them all.

I kicked off my shoes and climbed into the tub. I stretched out and picked up the remote, turned the television on and the volume down low. I flipped through the channels and imagined what it would be like to do this every night after Anastasia was in bed, only with water. I'd soak and I'd soak until I was a total prune.

"You have to go to both," I said. "As artists, they're completely different in many ways, but you'll also be able to see how Dalí's work was in part a reaction to Picasso's. And don't miss Miró while you're there, whether you're a big fan of Miró's work or not. It houses an incredible collection of contemporary art by other artists, too."

I slid down in the tub and tilted my head back. "Go, go. Go to every museum you can find. Just drink it all up, every single drop, because you can never really know for sure if you'll ever have the chance again. And when you finish with Miró, make sure—"

"Okay, thanks," the woman said. She hung up with a click before I could launch into my litany of regrets.

Even more than the museums, Seth and I had loved wandering the streets of Barcelona, from the harbor to the Gothic District, through the twisty, tree-lined avenues to the straight shot of Las Ramblas, listening to the tourists chattering, checking out the kiosks that sold everything from flowers to canaries. Our hostel was in a great location, a former pension within walking distance of just about everything. The shower stalls had doors, but no temperature control for the lukewarm water that dribbled out when you pushed a button. There was no hot water at all in the sinks and no power outlets in the big dormitory-style rooms.

Sheets cost extra, but when we'd arrived in Barcelona, we were both flush with money, me from the check I'd received just before I bailed from a job guiding Asian tours for an American company, Seth from a job he'd just quit teaching English in a Japanese school.

Breakfast with juice, coffee, cereal, and bread was served from seven-thirty to nine-thirty, so almost everybody was up and out of the hostel early. Seth and I would roam the streets for a while, looking for pieces of the Roman wall or examples of Gaudi architecture, but we'd circle back again and again to the hostel until we found our eight-bed room empty.

Because the best thing about this hostel was that each bed had a hospital-like curtain that pulled around it to create a small oasis of privacy. And you haven't really made love until you've made love in the middle of the morning in Barcelona.

I shook my head and picked up the remote from the edge of the tub. I started hunting for the volume button. Maybe it would drown out my entire memory bank.

Before I could find it, a male voice called out from the other side of the door.

"Hey, babe, I'm home," it said.

5

I JUMPED OUT OF CYNTHIA'S TUB FAST ENOUGH TO GET whiplash. I couldn't seem to fit my feet into my shoes, and when I tried to turn off the TV, the remote slid out of my hands and crashed into the tub. I dove for it and clicked off the TV, a hammering *shitshitshitshitshitshit* playing in my head.

I picked up my shoes and yanked the other bathroom door open. I literally slid on my socks out into the hallway, like a bad imitation of Tom Cruise in *Risky Business*. Fortunately I was wearing pants.

"Daddy, Daddy, Daddy," Cynthia's kids were yelling.

"What are you doing home?" Lexi, or maybe it was Treasure, said.

"Is it the weekend, Daddy?" Parker said.

I followed the sound of their voices, down the hallway, through the kitchen, to another hallway. I wondered if houses like this came with built-in GPS stations in case you lost your family.

Finally, I poked my head into an exercise room. Anastasia and the two other girls were jumping up and down on a row of three minitrampolines. Cynthia's husband was down on his hands and knees, and Parker was riding on his back.

"Faster, Daddy," Parker yelled. "Giddy-*yap*."

Cynthia's husband, Decker, looked up and smiled. He looked like the Pictionary definition of cute, rich husband: white button-down shirt with tie removed, top button open, sleeves rolled up. Premature five-o'clock shadow, gelled hair, blue eyes, brilliant white smile.

"Weren't you a blonde when I left this morning?" he said.

"Ha," I said. "Uh, um, Cynthia should be back any second."

"I've heard that one before," he said.

Treasure jumped off her trampoline and grabbed Parker by the back of the shirt. "Daddy, it's *my* turn."

Lexi jumped off hers and grabbed Treasure by the arm. "It's *my* turn, Daddy."

Anastasia was still jumping up and down. Her face was flushed and her ears were red, the way they sometimes got when she was too excited.

"Daddy," she yelled midjump. "It's *my* turn, Daddy."

The room went horribly, painfully quiet. Anastasia stopped jumping. Everybody stopped everything.

I knew I should say something, but I couldn't think of what.

Finally, Cynthia's husband reared up on his hind legs and neighed. He bucked Parker off his back. Lexi and Treasure lunged for him, but he shook them off and cantered over to Anastasia.

"Hop on, kiddo," he said.

I WAITED TILL Anastasia and I were sitting down to dinner to bring it up. I took a bite of the boxed macaroni and cheese I'd upgraded with fresh steamed broccoli. Anastasia loved broccoli. When she was a toddler, she used to call it *little trees*. She'd point to it from her high chair and say, "Mo little trees, please?"

She was a two-fisted broccoli eater back then. She'd hold a stalk in each chubby fist, and alternate bites from first one, then the other. Seth and I would smile at each other, enthralled by her sophisticated palate. Enthralled by her.

Tonight she picked at the food on her plate with a fork. Maybe it was just an overdose of Go-Gurt and Perrier.

I took a deep breath. "So," I said. "It must be hard sometimes to see the other kids with their dads."

She shrugged.

"It's okay to feel that way," I said.

"Duh," she said.

I let it go. I took a sip of my milk.

"Sometimes," I said, "what you know in your head and what you feel in your heart can be two different things."

Anastasia speared a piece of broccoli. "*Sometimes,*" she said to her plate, "kids have two mommies. *Sometimes* they have two daddies. *Sometimes* they don't have any parents at all. *Sometimes* they don't even have arms or legs."

My phone rang. Anastasia looked up.

I pushed the button. "Great Girlfriend Getaways," I said into the mouthpiece.

"Are you going to keep doing that for the rest of my life?" Anastasia said. She picked up her plate and headed for the living room.

I REPLAYED IT over and over again after Anastasia went to bed. Had I only made things worse? Obviously it had to be hard for her to see other kids with their dads. But, then again, one-parent families were practically the norm these days.

I did my best to be honest, matter-of-fact, and nonjudgmental when I talked about Seth, and I was pretty sure I'd pulled it off reasonably well, given the circumstances. I mean, what the hell do you say?

I told Anastasia Daddy had gone away, but it didn't mean he didn't love her. I told her he was in the Peace Corps, in Africa, and that made us sad, but he knew Mommy was taking good care of her. Actually, I only knew the Africa part secondhand, from Seth's parents, but I didn't tell her that.

I told Anastasia I didn't know if he'd be back, that sometimes grown-ups do things that don't make sense, and it's okay to be sad about it. That I was sad about it, but I knew we'd be okay without him. We were a team. We were fine. I'd always be there for her. Mommy wasn't going anywhere.

I knew I could have gotten Seth kicked out of the Peace Corps. It would only have taken a phone call. I could have gone after him for child support, too, which would probably also have gotten him kicked out of the Peace Corps, since I was pretty sure they wouldn't have taken him if they knew about Anastasia and me.

I could have done lots of things, but I just didn't. A part of me kept thinking he'd call, or he'd write, or he'd come home because he missed us, but he just didn't.

And the years went by.

The funny thing about life is that even the most unbearable things start to feel normal after a while. Hearts heal. Memories fade. Anastasia had a scrapbook filled with pictures of her dad that we kept on the bookcase next to the fireplace. I couldn't even remember the last time she'd taken it out to look at it.

She was fine. The daddy slip didn't mean a thing. She'd just gotten caught up in the moment. It meant she wanted a horsie ride, goddammit, not that she was desperate for a daddy. A daddy who would probably visit her twice before he took off and broke her heart again.

It was after nine, an hour past the end of my shift, and I realized I was still wearing my headphone. I took it off, threw it onto the kitchen counter, opened the refrigerator, closed it again.

I paced a lap around the living room. Then another.

Eventually I opened the door to Anastasia's room just a crack. She'd kicked the covers off and had one arm wrapped around the neck of her favorite stuffed animal, a monkey named Banana.

She still slept with the same night-light she'd had since birth. It was a cow jumping over the moon. I knew soon, very soon, she'd notice it and say it was a baby light. She'd insist on trading it for something covered in pink and purple daisies. And not long after that she'd declare a moratorium on night-lights of any kind.

But tonight it bathed her face in its soft yellow glow.

I tiptoed into her room and reached for her covers to pull them up, so she wouldn't wake up cold in the middle of the night. Her pink plaid diary was sprawled open on the sheet beside her, the key sticking out of its lock.

I picked it up.

I was so not the kind of mother who would ever snoop in her daughter's diary. But I did it anyway, standing in the hallway outside her bedroom, my heart beating wildly, because I knew my daughter would totally flip out if she caught me. Maybe most mothers eventually break their own code of ethics this way, and in our defense I would have to say it comes from the fiercest kind of love. The world is a tough place, and children are so terrifyingly fragile. Making sure your kid is okay trumps everything.

I'd only look at the last page—just a quick mom check. I flipped quickly through the blank lined pages in the back of the diary, listening for footsteps from Anastasia's room.

And then I came to this:

Did you have to go away?

All I do is miss you all day long

Do you have to stay so long?

6

WHEN I GOT TO STARBUCKS, BILLY SANDERS AND TWO venti cappuccinos were waiting at the same table we'd sat at last time.

He stood up, put his palms together, and bowed.

I burst out laughing.

"*What*?" he said.

He was wearing a knee-length red silk kimono, tied around the waist with a white obi that matched his sneakers.

I knew it was unprofessional, but I couldn't seem to stop laughing. My eyes were tearing, and I was gasping for breath. When I tried to get myself under control, I made a sound that was a cross between a neigh and a snort.

"Nice," he said.

"Sorry." I cleared my throat.

"Tell me you didn't ride your bike in that," I said. I bit down on my lower lip so I wouldn't lose it all over again.

He held out my chair. "Why, is there some sort of Japanese bicycle/kimono rule I should know about?"

I burst out laughing all over again. Most of Starbucks was looking at us. I sat down fast and reached for my cappuccino.

"*Not* that it's any of your business," Billy Sanders whispered, "but I'm wearing bike shorts under it." He raised an eyebrow. "Matching."

I put my head on the table. "Stop," I said. "Please stop."

Finally I lifted up my head.

"So," I said. I reached for my folder.

"So," he said. He handed me a check. "Nice to see you laugh, even if it was at me. You were pretty uptight last time."

"Excuse me?" I said.

He smiled. "I know uptight when I see it."

He had one of those vast, infectious smiles that probably made everyone he met want to hang out with him. I thought there might even be a little spark between us, but it had been so long since I'd been in such close proximity to a man, albeit one wearing a kimono with bike shorts, I could easily be hallucinating. If I had the extra energy, or could even remember how to flirt, I might have considered testing the waters. "Okay," I said. "First thing. I hope you saved the receipt on that kimono. . . ."

Billy took a sip of his cappuccino. "I don't know what the problem is. It worked for David Bowie in *Ziggy Stardust*."

"It makes you look like a total weeaboo."

He crossed his legs, and I got a little peek of his red bike shorts. He had amazing thighs, wiry and muscular. Must have been all that bike riding.

"A whatahoo?" he said.

"A weeaboo. It's short for 'wannabee Japanese.' You know, someone who wears manga T-shirts, lives on ramen noodles, and bows a lot."

"Hey, I only bowed once. But I see your point. Kind of geeky, huh?"

I smiled. "Historically, it's geek meets goth."

"You mean the vampire kids?"

"No, goths and vampires both wear black, but goths smoke and drink, while vampires are actually healthy, at least the New Bloods inspired by *Twilight*. They're more into drinking to-mato juice and pretending it's blood. All of this, by the way, is

simply an extension of the whole jock-versus-stoner thing from our own high school days."

"Wow," he said. "Remind me to hire you again when my kids get a little older."

My stomach fell like a descending elevator missing a floor. I hadn't realized how much I'd been kind of hoping that Billy Sanders was single. I glanced at the ring finger of his left hand.

He saw me do it. I looked away quickly.

"Divorced," he said.

"Excuse me?" I said. I could feel a blush burning my face. I flipped my hair out from behind my ears to camouflage it.

"You were looking at my ring finger," he said.

"No, I wasn't," I said.

"See," he said. He adjusted the front of his kimono. "You *are* uptight."

"Well, compared to a guy who wears a red kimono in broad daylight, who wouldn't be?"

We stared at each other.

"How many kids do you have?" I finally said.

"Two. Both boys."

"I have one daughter."

He gave my ring finger an exaggerated look. "Anybody else in the family?"

I actually giggled. "Just us," I said, and for the first time in a long time it didn't feel like such a bad thing.

WHEN I GOT TO the Great Girlfriend Getaways office, Joni Robertson pushed herself up from her chair to give me a big hug. Her coarse gray hair smelled like violets, and hugging her always made me think of homemade bread just out of the oven.

She pushed me away to get a good look. "You hangin' in there, kid?"

I nodded. "How 'bout you?"

"Don't ask." She pushed me away and headed for her desk. She was wearing jeans and a Great Girlfriend Getaways T-shirt with a hip new pair of Skechers Shape-ups. Joni was well into her seventies, solid and vibrant in a matter-of-fact way that sometimes inspired me, and other times made me wonder if I'd ever get there myself.

I pulled up a chair and took out a small notebook. "Okay, what do you need?"

She scrolled through some files on her computer. "That snippy little Kiki just quit on me. Can you pick up her four-to-midnight tonight? I'll try to get someone else in place by her next shift."

"Got it. What else?"

"That new resort we're using in St. John wants to exchange Web site banner links. Can you whip up something for them—logo, hyperlink, plus something fun and girlfriendy?"

I made a note. "Of course."

Joni nodded. She scrolled for a while longer, then stopped and looked at me over her zebra-striped reading glasses. "Hey, you don't want to jump in on that Costa Rican surfing trip, do you? I think we might need another set of hands. It's only six days."

It was positively Pavlovian the way I could feel myself salivate. Six days in Costa Rica. Sun and surf and an optional side trip to the rain forest. I could picture myself sprawled in a hammock on my hotel patio . . . sipping a drink out by the pool . . . curled up in my hotel room with a good book.

I could even see myself hanging ten on a surfboard, not that I'd ever surfed before. But Joni would hire a local expert

for that. He'd be tall and toned, with narrow hips and broad, salty shoulders. . . .

I shook it off. "You know I can't," I said.

Joni took off her glasses and cleaned them with her T-shirt. "Anastasia can stay with me. She'll be fine. And so will you."

"It's too much," I said. I wasn't sure if I meant it was too much to ask of Joni, or too much for me to handle. Maybe both.

Joni gave me a long look. "Okay," she said finally. "Just let me know when you're ready."

"Thanks," I said.

Joni was more than a boss. She was my friend. When Seth abandoned Anastasia and me, I'd pulled away from just about everybody. Maybe I was embarrassed or even ashamed, or maybe I just felt that I no longer had anything in common with ordinary people. Joni filled the gap. Nothing shocked her, and she knew when to push and when to leave me alone.

I opened my mouth to tell Joni that Seth was back. Then I closed it again. I wasn't sure I wanted to hear what she would say. I had this strange, irrational feeling, as if even the tiniest movement I made in any direction would trigger a series of events that could only lead to a train wreck.

I wanted to dig a nice, safe hole in the sand, just big enough to hold my daughter and me. We'd stay there until Seth blew by again, until Anastasia was older and stronger and safely grown up. We'd get through pierced ears and prom, camp and college. Once I was sure Anastasia had picked the right life partner, someone strong and reliable, we'd give Seth a quick call and he could walk her down the aisle.

Maybe.

7

WHEN ANASTASIA AND I OPENED THE DOOR TO GO OUT TO
wait for the bus, Cynthia and her kids were walking toward us
dragging two wooden porch railings.

"Here you go," Cynthia said.

She and Parker placed their railing up against my house.
Then Cynthia took the second railing from Lexi and Treasure,
and rested it up against the first one. The kids ran off to wait for
the bus.

The railings were made of white-painted wood, chunky
and simple, and exactly what I would have replaced my rusty
metal railings with if I could have afforded to.

"What are those for?" I asked.

Cynthia inspected her fingernails for chips. "Up to you,
but I was thinking maybe earrings."

"Cute," I said. "Where did you get them?"

"I just told my client she should beef up her railings a little.
Piece of pie."

"How do you know they'll fit?"

Cynthia winked. "I measured first, of course. After all, I
am a professional."

It finally sank in. "Ohmigod," I said. "You have a client?"

Cynthia's face lit up. She did a dance that involved circling
her hips in her tennis skirt while she stirred an imaginary vat.
"I have a client," she sang. "I have a client. I have a *cli*-ent."

By the time she finished her song, the bus had already pulled away. I felt a sharp stab of guilt, as if I'd let Anastasia down by not watching over her until the last possible second. I closed my eyes and tried to visualize her surrounded by a soft white protective light all the way to school.

When I opened my eyes, Cynthia was walking away.

"Thanks for the railings," I yelled.

She waved one hand over her head, twisting her wrist back and forth, the jewels in her tennis bracelet glistening in the morning sun.

I SPENT THE MORNING designing a Great Girlfriends Getaway banner link for the St. John resort Web site. I really just needed a quick peek at the site to make sure my design would jump out, but also feel like it belonged. But I found myself browsing each and every page, imagining what it would be like to stretch out on all that white sand and snorkel in the turquoise waters.

At first, the sand and the sea were enough, but after a while I needed some companionship. So I pictured a man rubbing sunscreen on my back with strong, sure hands. I tried to turn, just enough to get a look at him, but he stayed out of sight. Then I tried turning him into Billy, but I couldn't get him out of his red kimono and into a bathing suit, so as a fantasy, it was only moderately successful.

I forced myself to focus. I finished the banner ad and sent it off to Joni. Then I moved on to designing business cards for Billy to take with him to Japan. If I ordered them right away through the online print service I used, I'd get them in time for our next meeting.

I stayed with it, experimenting with fonts and colors, adding a photo of the Akira bike, until I had a card design that I
thought would be just what he needed. I placed the order, using the one credit card I allowed myself. Then I got to work on
the invoice, adding in a design fee and marking up the cards to
what he'd pay at his local office supply store. If I had a few more
Billy Sanders on my client list, I might actually be able to afford
to hire someone to install my new porch railings.

All morning I'd been trying to keep myself from going into
Anastasia's room, but it turned out that reading one page in
your daughter's diary was a lot like trying to eat one potato chip.

"Okay, just one more," I said out loud. I pushed myself
away from the desk in the office area I'd made out of one end of
my bedroom. As I walked by my bed on the way out, I grabbed
my faded green comforter and pulled it up to meet the pillows
in an underachieving attempt to make the bed.

For the first year or so after Anastasia and I moved in, I'd
made my bed every day, so happy to actually own the room that
surrounded it. But it got harder and harder to care about a room
that no other adult saw. Now dirty clothes littered the floor,
and two half-full glasses of water kept each other company on
my bedside table.

Anastasia had made her bed this morning, as she'd done
pretty much every morning since we'd moved in. Three evenly
spaced purple and pink fake fur pillows, and a throng of stuffed
animals, rested against her headboard.

I checked under the pillows, peeked under the twin bed,
and found Anastasia's diary wedged between the mattress and
the box spring. I could feel the hard plastic eyes of the stuffed
animals on me.

"*What*?" I said.

They stared back, silently judging me. I looked around the
room, wondering if it were possible that my daughter had some-

how gotten her hands on a hidden camera. Maybe Cynthia's kids had given her one of their extra nanny cams.

I couldn't handle staying in Anastasia's room, but I couldn't seem to stop myself from snooping either, so I carried the diary out to the hallway.

The diary was locked. I went back to my bedroom office and grabbed one of the paper clips I kept in a mug with a broken handle. I sat down at my desk, straightened out one end of the paper clip, and wiggled it around until the lock gave. It was ridiculously easy. I wasn't sure if that made me feel better or worse.

To dispose of the evidence, I buried the paper clip in the wastebasket under my desk. I stayed in my office chair and started flipping back to front through the little pink diary. I closed my eyes when I got to the poem I'd already seen. It was just too painful to read it again.

I skimmed an entry about how Anastasia wanted to sit with Becca on the bus, but she couldn't because Becca was already sitting with Alle, who usually sat with Storie. I breathed a shallow sigh of relief, then flipped to another page.

I wish my father was President O'Bama, the first line said.

I smiled. So cute that she'd made the president Irish with that apostrophe. I breathed a half sigh of relief. It was starting to look like Anastasia was simply in the throes of some kind of normal, developmental daddy stage. Every ten-year-old in the country probably wished the president could be her father.

I kept reading. *Then Melia and Sasha would be my sisters and we could share things. My room in the white house would be pink. Unless it had to be white. That would be ok if I could keep my pillows and stuff animals. My mom would have servents to answer the phone.*

My eyes teared up. I wasn't sure where we would stash Michelle O'Bama, but how sweet that Anastasia had thought to give me someone to answer the phone. Although maybe that was more about her being embarrassed by my headphone than about me being overworked.

I slid down to the floor of the hallway and turned a few more pages until I came to this:

Forgot all about me

Away in the Peach Core

Teaching kids who need him more

Helping kids in Africa get

Extra help on their home work

Really need him to come home and help me do mine

I jumped up as if I'd been stung by a bee. I slammed the little pink book closed and locked it, while I jogged out to the hallway and back into Anastasia's room. I shoved the diary under her mattress as fast as I could and raced through my house. I pushed my screen door open so hard it crashed into the side of the house.

I grabbed one of my old rusty metal railings with both hands and yanked.

It didn't budge.

I kicked it with one foot, then the other, like some psycho mom practicing her karate moves. Nothing happened, so I just kept kicking until I couldn't kick anymore. Then I grabbed the railing with both hands and started rocking it back and forth, and back and forth, as hard and as fast as I could.

I wasn't sure exactly when I started to scream, but somewhere during the second set of karate kicks, I realized that I was letting out a loud yell with every kick.

"I hate you," I yelled. "I hate you. I hate you. I hate you. I hate you."

When Cynthia came out of her house, I was dripping with sweat and tired, just so tired. I crossed my arms over my chest and tried not to cry.

She pulled her bangs across her forehead as she walked. "Wow," she said. "You're such a Jill of all trades."

"Yeah, right," I said. I gave the railing a pathetic little kick. It didn't move. I wiped one eye and then the other with the backs of my hands.

"Not to worry, girlfriend," Cynthia said. "I have power tools. I'll be right back."

She took a few steps in the direction of her house, then stopped and turned around. "Oh, wait," she said. Her hand was still on her forehead, as if she had a serious headache. She wasn't the only one. "First I have a couple of tiny calls to make, and then I'll be right back."

As soon as Cynthia was out of sight, I went into my kitchen to call Seth. There was no way around it. They might eventually knock my railings down, but all the karate kicks and power tools in the world couldn't change the fact that my daughter needed her father, and I had no choice but to let him back into our lives.

8

WE WERE HEADING FOR *MEHICO*. ALL FIFTEEN WOMEN AND three men gathered around the ancient kitchen, watching me unload my grocery bags, as if I were about to pull a rabbit out of my hat.

"Today," I said, "we'll be celebrating Cinco de Mayo."

"But it's only Tres de Mayo," Ethel said. She was wearing a wild salmon-colored sweat suit that worked well with her *I Love Lucy* hair. She'd drawn thick orange lips over her much thinner ones, and I couldn't stop looking at the places where she'd colored outside the lines.

"Close enough," T-shirt Tom said. Not that he could see it through the fingerprints on his glasses, but today's shirt read WISH YOU WERE BEER. I had to admit I kind of agreed with the sentiment. Maybe I should have tried to smuggle in some Dos Equis, to take the edge off while keeping the class culturally accurate.

I took a quick peek at the doorway, then pulled my attention back to the group.

"Cinco de Mayo," I continued as I placed a measuring cup on the pitted counter, "celebrates the victory of the historic battle of 1863 between *Mehico* and France. The holiday is a symbol of Mexican pride and unity, and it includes lots of fun festivities."

I reached into a large plastic bag and pulled out a piñata.

"Oooh," the whole class said in one big breath.

The piñata was a tricolored papier-mâché donkey. To make up for the fact that I'd ordered it online from Oriental Trading, I told the group that the origin of the piñata dates back to centuries before the arrival of the first Spanish explorers on Mexican soil, and that Mexican Indians made piñatas from fragile earthenware jars painted to look like favorite gods.

It was a beautiful spring day. Sunlight poured through the tall windows of the kitchen, but I couldn't seem to keep warm. I rubbed my hands together and took another quick glance at the empty doorway. As soon as Anastasia had left for school this morning, I'd jumped into the shower. For some ridiculous reason, I'd even shaved my legs and taken the time to slather on copious amounts of Vaseline Intensive Care.

I'd put on a white T-shirt and a gauzy navy skirt with an embroidered lace hem I'd bought on clearance two years ago at Anthropologie, not because I was dressing up, of course, but because my legs were too sticky for pants. I glanced down now and saw a big glob of lotion between two toes. I bent down and tried to rub it away.

They watched my every move. "Don't we look pretty today, honey," Ethel said when I finished rubbing. "New boyfriend?"

I could feel myself blush. I flipped my hair out from behind my ears and caught the scent of my Suave Tropical Coconut Shampoo.

"Authentic Mexican corn tortillas," I said, "are made with a specially treated corn flour called masa harina." I hadn't been able to get my hands on fresh masa, which needs to be used right away, but I'd found some dried masa at the third supermarket I tried.

Making tortillas from scratch turned out to be a lot harder than it sounded. We added water to the masa harina and made dough, then divided the dough into small balls. I picked one up and flattened it with a rolling pin on a cutting board sprinkled with more masa. I peeled it off and tried to maneuver the paper-thin circle into one of the prehistoric skillets that had been heating on the stove.

The knuckles of both hands grazed the bottom of the skillet. "Shit," I yelled, as I threw the tortilla-to-be up in the air.

Several women went into Florence Nightingale mode and circled around me.

"Are we in Italy now?" T-shirt Tom said. "Get it? Pizza?"

Good thing I'd brought store-bought tortillas for backup. The class kicked into gear while I ran my hands under cold water.

One of the women scraped my aborted tortilla off the counter and started rolling out another masa ball. The others divided into groups. I'd found fresh asparagus on sale and steamed it last night, so one group cut it into one-inch pieces and added goat cheese and chopped cilantro. Another group shredded cooked chicken and mixed in black beans and tomato.

Ethel and her friends tore open the bags of Trader Joe's Lite Mexican Blend shredded cheese, and another woman snipped open the packets of Wholly Guacamole. The class formed a long line and took turns spooning ingredients onto the tortillas. Then they moved on to the other frying pans, working quickly and efficiently, as if they'd been working together at a quesadilla factory most of their lives.

"I got one!" the woman attempting to make tortillas finally yelled. She flipped her masa-made tortilla onto a paper plate and held it up for everyone to see. The class applauded, even though it was shaped like an amoeba and riddled with holes.

I turned off the water and blotted my hands carefully with scratchy brown paper towels. They might be good for the environment, but they sure were a bitch on your blisters. I opened the bag of assorted candy and started stuffing the piñata. The early eaters came over to help me. When we finished, I stood on a chair and hung the donkey from one of the dusty fluorescent lights in the middle of the room, trying to ignore my throbbing hands.

After everybody finished eating and we packed up the leftovers, we formed a circle around the piñata. Each of the students took a blindfolded turn whacking at the donkey with the handle of a broom, while everybody else jumped out of the way.

I wondered what the liability issues were for giving weapons to blindfolded seniors.

"Take this, you ass," Ethel yelled when it was her turn.

Everybody cheered. A few of the women did the Macarena while Ethel whacked away.

Eventually we made it around the circle, piñata still intact.

"Your turn, Jill honey," a nice woman named Bev said.

I was an expert. Anastasia had had a piñata at all ten of her birthday parties, even when it was handmade and only the two of us. I felt for the donkey with the point of the broom handle, then traced my way up and down the length of its body until I found the soft spot.

I jabbed upward, merely grazing my target. I readjusted the angle of the broom handle. I remembered the first piñata I'd barely managed to hang by myself after Seth had taken off. With each passing year, I'd become more proficient. I was strong. I was invincible.

I let out a roar and thrust upward as hard as I could. Hard candy rained down on my head, surprisingly painful.

"Whoa, baby," T-shirt Tom said. Somebody whistled. The class broke into cheers and applause.

When I pulled off my blindfold, Seth was standing in the doorway.

Ethel reached for my broomstick, as if she were afraid I might ride off on it. "I knew it was a boyfriend," she whispered through her orange lips.

"SEE YOU NEXT WEEK," I called, in what I hoped was a peppy, optimistic voice.

"Where are we going next time?" T-shirt Tom asked, probably so he could choose a coordinating shirt.

"You'll have to wait and see-eee," I managed to say, though I could feel the words sticking in my throat.

Just about everyone stopped to bend down and grab a handful of candy on the way out the door. Too late, I remembered the paper lunch bags Anastasia had helped me paint in bright fiesta colors to use as candy bags.

A few of my students stopped to talk to Seth as they passed him.

"Nice to meet you, honey," Bev said, even though she hadn't.

"You, too," Seth said.

Ethel fluffed her orange hair as she walked by. "Take good care of our Jill."

"She's a real catch, that one," T-shirt Tom said. One of his sidekicks nodded.

"Mmm," Seth said noncommittally.

When the last student was gone, I glanced in his direction, keeping my eyes just to the side of his face.

"Sit," I said.

Seth sat. He chose a place way down at the opposite end of the long rickety table, about as far away from me as he could possibly get, not counting Africa.

I took my time picking up the last of the candy. Finally, I stood up and actually looked at him. His hair was still long, but it had been recently cut. He was wearing dark dress pants and a white button-down shirt with sage green pinstripes. And shoes, shiny leather ones that tied and everything.

I took a moment to blow on my blistering knuckles.

"Are you okay?" he asked.

I looked at him. "A little late to be asking that, don't you think?"

He took a deep breath and gripped the edge of the table. "Okay, let's get it over with," he said. "Just say it. All of it. Get it all out."

"Right," I said. "You take off for seven years, I yell at you for seven seconds, and we're even."

He stared at me with flat eyes. "Then tell me what you want me to do. Whatever it is, I'll do it."

I wanted him to find a way to rewind the last seven years, to make it all go away. I wanted to wake up together on a lazy weekend morning in our old apartment, with the most beautiful little three-year-old in the world. I wanted to curl up in bed together and read the Sunday paper, while Anastasia colored all over the comics with her new fat crayons.

Seth was the official weekend breakfast cook, so eventually he'd get up and make pancakes on the secondhand griddle we'd found at a flea market. Not just any pancakes, but pancake works of art. For Anastasia, it might be pancake circles linked together to create Minnie Mouse ears, with sliced banana eyes and a frozen blueberry smile. Maybe a big pancake heart for me, covered in blueberry bumps. Seth was endlessly creative, and the best part of breakfast was not knowing whether he'd come back with a family of pancake dinosaurs or a bouquet of pancake flowers.

"Good job, Daddy," Anastasia would say, and we'd all dig in. Eating breakfast in bed with a toddler was a messy proposition, but blueberry-stained sheets seemed a small price to pay for mornings like that.

What I wanted, what I really, really wanted, was for Seth to find the place and the time—the exact moment—right before he decided to leave us. Then I wanted him to make a different decision, so we could still be a family, and I wouldn't have to hate him for the rest of my natural life.

I looked down at the blisters on my knuckles. Anastasia was ten, and my hands were already starting to look old. I turned one hand over and found what I thought might be my life line. About halfway across my hand, it broke off completely. There was only a small, unbroken space before a new line picked up, but I wasn't sure I had it in me to take the leap of faith to get there.

My eyes filled up. I looked up at the ceiling to keep the tears from spilling out. I wished Seth dead. Just for a second, and not enough to impale him on a broomstick like the ass that he was, but with all my heart, my entire bruised and broken heart. It was the only solution I could think of. Short of widowhood, there was simply no way to keep Seth out of my life and still be a good mother.

I blinked until the tears were gone.

I lowered my head and cleared my throat. "Okay," I said. "This is what I want you to do. I want you to visit your daughter. I want you to do it exactly when and where I tell you to, and I want you to be precisely on time. And if you ever miss a single visit or let her down in any way . . ."

I looked him right in the eyes, trying to see into his soul.

". . . I promise you, Seth, I'll hunt you down. And this time I swear to God I'll kill you."

He looked at me for a long time.

"Got it," he finally said.

9

"WOW," BILLY SAID. "NICE JOB." HE POINTED TO THE レンタサイクル that was centered in red at the top of the card. "What does *that* mean?"

I flipped the card over and held it so he could see. BICYCLE RENTALS it said in red in the exact same place.

I handed him the card. His hand brushed mine just before I let go, and I felt a little shock that must have been static electricity. My hair probably had little flyaway pieces sticking straight up, too. I smoothed it down with both hands, just in case.

Billy turned the card over again and traced his finger along the レンタサイクル. "Bicycle rentals," he said. "Cool. How do you pronounce it?"

"Re-n-ta-sa-i-ku-ru," I said.

"Re-n-ta-sa-i-ku-ru," he repeated.

His raccoon eyes met mine, and I felt the same little electrical current charging the air between us. It was hard to tell whether I was actually attracted to him or whether that saying about a woman without a man being like a fish without a bicycle was just plain wrong. Maybe there's always a little jolt when female electricity comes in close proximity to male electricity that is even close to the same frequency. Did electricity have frequency? If the man already has a bicycle, does the woman get stuck with the fish? Did other people have these crazy, off-topic thoughts when they were supposed to be working?

"Re-n-ta-sa-i-ku-ru," Billy said again. "Am I saying it right?"

"Perfectly," I said.

"Come with me to Japan," he said.

Apparently I wasn't the only person having crazy, rambling thoughts. I burst out laughing.

He shook his head. "Here we go again."

I totally lost it. I couldn't seem to stop laughing.

He raised an eyebrow. "Do you do this often?"

"Sorry," I said. "I'm really sorry. I never do this." I reached for a napkin and wiped my eyes. "I can't even remember the last time I really laughed."

"Well, that's too bad. It certainly becomes you."

"Thank you," I said, not because I necessarily believed him, but because it was the most professional way to respond to a compliment. I took a sip of my cappuccino.

He took a sip of his. It left a frothy mustache, as if he'd just signed for a *Got Milk?* commercial. When he wiped it off, I kind of missed it.

"What?" he said.

I shook my head. "Nothing."

"Okay, back to Japan. I think it's a perfectly reasonable idea for you to come with me. You know the culture, you speak Japanese. . . ."

"Ha," I said. " 'Good morning,' 'good afternoon,' and 'bicycle rental,' which by the way, I found on the Internet. Maybe five other words if I'm lucky. That's worth a plane ticket to Tokyo?"

I reached into my folder and placed the invoice on top of the box of business cards. "Okay," I said. "The business cards will be extremely important for establishing your credentials in Japan. Once we find the go-between, we'll have him double-check these just to be sure they're perfect."

Billy nodded.

"Always present the card after the bow or handshake—just follow their lead as to which one is appropriate. And make sure you present it with the Japanese side facing the person you're meeting, because they'll want to read it on the spot."

Billy was still nodding, his head going up and down rhythmically, like one of those cute bobble head figures on the dashboard of somebody's car.

I closed my eyes to get him off my dashboard, then opened them again. "Okay, then, when you're given a card, ask your go-between to help you pronounce the name on the card so you can greet the card giver, and also to help you figure out the appropriate thing to say, based on the situation. And be absolutely sure you handle any card you're given with the utmost care and respect. Don't just shove it in your pocket, especially if it's a back pocket, and . . ."

He stopped nodding and grinned. "And make sure I don't scratch an itch with it, particularly if the itch is near my back pocket?"

I smiled. "And heaven forbid, don't pick your teeth with it."

He leaned forward over the table. "You know, it's suddenly hitting me that I probably insult someone from another culture every time I walk down the street."

"I wouldn't worry too much. It's nice to be aware, but the onus is pretty much on the person stepping into the other culture."

"When in Rome, do as the Romans do?"

"To a degree," I said. "Though the Romans also have a responsibility to make their guests feel comfortable. The classic story goes that when the shah of Persia visited Queen Victoria, he picked up his finger bowl and drank from it. Queen Victoria didn't miss a beat. She just drank from *her* finger bowl, and everybody at the table followed suit."

"So that's how we all started drinking out of our finger bowls."

"Precisely," I said. I opened my eyes wide. "Wow, you're such a quick study."

He grinned. "Why, thank you," he said. "I have to tell you, this is the first time I've thought any of this stuff was the least bit interesting. I always thought etiquette was just a bunch of uptight rules. I bet you're a great person to travel with, like having your own personal Emily Post *and* Fodor with you at all times. How did your marriage break up anyway?"

The question caught me midsip, and my cappuccino took a wrong turn on its way down my throat. I started to choke, and the harder I tried to stop it, the worse it got.

Billy jumped up and ran to the barista counter. By the time he came back with a paper cup filled with water, I was relatively under control.

I took a small sip.

"Okay now?"

I nodded. "Sorry," I said. "But that was *so* not a guy question."

"*What?*" he said. "Guys aren't allowed to talk about what happened to a marriage in this culture?"

I thought for a moment. "Only if they go first."

"Fair enough." Billy stretched back in his chair. "Pretty basic," he said. "We never should have been together in the first place. I'd spend my whole life outdoors if I could. Biking, swimming, surfing, running, hiking, climbing, skiing, skating, sledding, snowmobiling, you name it. My ex is afraid of everything—mountains, planes, highways, fresh air, Portuguese men-of-war."

"Portuguese men-of-war?"

"Yeah, you know, those jellyfish?"

"Actually," I said, "they're not really jellyfish. They're siphonophores, animals made up of a colony of organisms that work together."

"Jeez, what don't you know? Anyway, whatever they are, she was so afraid a school of them would show up and sting her, she wouldn't even dip a toe in the water. Not even in a swimming pool. Her idea of a good time is to stay inside and knit."

"Wow," I said, because I couldn't think of anything else.

He smiled. "It wasn't all bad. I got some nice sweaters out of the deal. And two great sons. They're both fearless—and, man, can they knit."

"How often do you see them?" I asked. He seemed like a good father, but I still hoped it wasn't too often. I needed to know that these things could be worked out, but without rocking the boat too much. Especially a boat I'd kept afloat by myself for so long.

"Oh," Billy said. "They live with me. Well, most of the time. Actually they go back and forth whenever they want. I bought out my wife's half of the house so the boys wouldn't have to move, then about a year later she and her current husband bought the house two doors down. It works out great."

I looked at him in horror. In a million years, I couldn't imagine ever getting there.

"What?" he said.

"How do you handle it? I mean, how can you stand to be so goddamned civilized?"

He grinned his big grin. "That's pretty funny coming from an etiquette guru. If you think about it, the world of divorce is a culture just like any other."

I wondered if it would be too obvious if I took out a pen and wrote that down. Maybe I could meditate on it later.

"But," I said, "didn't you ever want to, I don't know, *kill* your ex-wife?"

He shrugged. "Nah. Well, maybe in the beginning. But, here's the thing, we had these two incredible kids together, and no matter what, we're always going to be connected to each other through them. So, essentially, we divorced each other but stayed family. Maybe we're a little like those siphon . . . whatever they're called."

"Siphonophores."

"Thank you. Siphonophores. We're separate, but we all still clump together."

My head suddenly felt like it weighed five hundred pounds. I put my elbows on the table so I could rest it in my hands. "And it doesn't bother you that she's married to someone else?"

"Not usually. When it gets to me, I just imagine him naked. Jeez, could that guy use a trip to the gym."

I sat up straight again and pulled my stomach in.

"Sorry, that was beneath me. He's actually a nice guy. And the two of them take the boys to all kinds of places you couldn't drag me to. I mean, the symphony? Spare me. I'm fine with the music part, but let me listen to it on my iPod while I'm out riding on a beautiful day, thank you very much."

I tried to imagine what might have happened if Seth had been more like Billy. Maybe he would have just come to me one day and told me that it was nothing personal, we simply had nothing in common.

But we did.

It wasn't only Anastasia. We'd had everything in common. At least I'd thought we did. Maybe it wasn't all candlelit dinners and walks on the beach, but I mean, what marriage was? We were in love, and we even liked each other, too. There was still a large box up in the attic with proof of our shared adventures—a chipped Tube map mug we'd picked up at a transport museum gift shop in London's Covent Garden, a miniature Tour Eiffel we'd loved for its cheap metal tackiness, a mortar and pestle carved from a solid piece of "peacefully collected oak" and etched with a Celtic trinity knot, a partial set of celadon-glazed sake cups, dog-eared copies of outdated Michelin Green Guides, and an old T-shirt that said YOU BETTER BELIZE IT, which I stopped wearing and made into a pillow before it fell apart. I couldn't stand to look at them, but I couldn't bear to throw them out.

Billy cleared his throat. "Hey, do you have time to go somewhere and grab a late lunch?"

I looked at my watch. "Ohmigod," I said. "I had no idea it was this late."

I was already halfway to the door by the time he caught up. "Was it something I said?" he said.

"The bus," I said. I lunged for the door, then made a dash for my car.

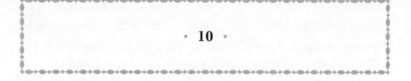

ANASTASIA PICKED UP A ROUNDED TRIANGLE OF CHICKEN and black bean quesadilla with her fingers and dipped a corner into the dollop of Wholly Guacamole on her plate.

When the phone rang, I took a quick bite of my own quesadilla.

"Great Girlfriend Getaways," I said into my headphone. "Feisty and fabulous man-free escapes both close to home and all over the world. When was the last time you got together with *your* girlfriends?"

"It's Seth."

I looked at Anastasia. She was chewing away happily. We'd had the asparagus and goat cheese quesadillas for dinner last night, and I hadn't been sure Lunch Around the World leftovers would fly two nights in a row.

"What's your question?" I said in a singsong voice.

Anastasia picked up her plate and started heading in the direction of the living room.

"You haven't told her yet?" Seth said into one ear.

"Not your business," I whispered.

With my other ear, I heard the TV click on in the living room.

"Our Costa Rica trip is available with or without surfing," I said loudly. "But our surfing instructor is not only extremely good-looking, he's also lots of fun. And he's great with beginners, so we strongly encourage you and your girlfriends to give him, I mean *it*, a try."

"I'm calling to double-check on Sunday," Seth said. His voice was flat. "Five o'clock, right?"

Everything in me wanted to find a way to wiggle out of it—virus, birthday party, impending tsunami, whatever it took.

"Right," I said.

"Can I bring anything?" he asked politely, as if he were simply an old friend coming by for dinner.

"Yeah," I said. "Seven years of child support."

He didn't say anything.

I found the disconnect button on my cell phone and pushed it.

Anastasia came back and sat down at the table. "Who was that?" she asked.

Little pitchers have big ears my mother would have said. It was actually one of the few things I could still remember her saying.

She hadn't been much of a mother. Or maybe it was just that she didn't really need much from anybody, so she assumed I didn't either. My mother was her own best company. Her idea of a good time was to pop a Swanson's chicken pot pie in the oven for each of us and curl up with a good book until the timer went off.

We didn't go to church, or museums, or movies, and she didn't invite friends over. She went to her secretarial job, came home, got up the next day, and did it all over again. On weekends she just spent more time reading.

Pictures of my father were the only things that brightened up our two-bedroom apartment. He'd died before I turned two, but I'd memorized his smile from the photos—two on the bookcase in the living room, one on my mother's bedside table.

I'd managed to convince myself that I could remember him not only picking me up, but also throwing me up in the air and catching me as I giggled my way back down into his arms. He seemed fun and nice and handsome, but more than that, even in photos he seemed alive, so much more alive than my mother.

As soon as I was old enough, I spent most of my energy trying to attach myself to other families. Big, messy families with lots of kids and noise. Families who sat down at long dinner tables together, instead of eating in front of the television on two little fold-out TV tables. Families who piled their kids into the station wagon and went skating or bowling or to the drive-in.

As I headed into my teenage years, other girls my age started choosing their friends based on social status or shared interests, but I continued to pick mine for their families. And then I tried to wiggle my way in and blend like a chameleon, hoping against hope that they wouldn't notice me and make me go home.

I studied hard, mostly to avoid having to live a boring life like my mother. I knew I wanted a fascinating career, but beyond that, things got a little bit vague. I thought maybe I'd become some new hybrid, a little bit Jane Goodall, only I'd study people instead of primates, and a whole lotta Margaret Mead, but with a less complicated personal life. They were the role models I wanted my mother to be. Sometimes I'd imagine that I'd grown up a wild child frolicking with Jane and the apes. Once in college I caught myself just before I told a classmate Margaret Mead was my great-aunt.

As set as I was on a big career, I also couldn't wait to fill my life with a family of my own. My husband would come from a big, boisterous clan, with zillions of cousins. I'd been thrilled when Seth's family fit the bill. But they'd all drifted away after Seth took off. Or maybe I'd pulled away.

Nature or nurture, a family larger than two seemed miles beyond my reach.

"Mom?" Anastasia said. "Who *was* that?"

She put her plate on the table and reached for her pink headband. I looked at my beautiful daughter, her trusting almond eyes, the dusting of freckles across her nose. Her father's freckles.

I had absolutely no idea how to handle this. I picked up a piece of chicken and black bean quesadilla, then put it down again. "No one," I said. "Just a work call."

After we cleared our dinner dishes and placed them in the rickety old dishwasher, Anastasia tore a piece of lined paper from her notebook and placed it on the table. She flipped through her spelling book until she'd found this week's words, all with a silent *e* at the end. Her teacher gave a pretest on Monday and a final test on Friday. The homework was to practice every night in between.

I'd had the exact same homework assignment at Anastasia's age. My mother taught me to fold a sheet of paper lengthwise, then write my spelling words in a long column on one side. To practice, I'd look at each word, memorize it, and flip the paper over to test myself as I wrote it from memory. My mother read her book on the sofa in the next room.

Anastasia picked up her favorite pen, pink with a fluff of purple feathers on the top. She tickled her nose with it while she waited for the first word.

"Ready?" I said.

She nodded.

"Okay," I said. "*Struggle*. Sometimes mothers struggle to know the right thing to do."

"*Struggle*," Anastasia said as she wrote. "Sometimes kids struggle to wake up in the morning."

"*Bruise*," I said. "When you've been hurt, a bruise can take a long, long time to go away."

"*Bruise*," Anastasia said. "When you get a bruise, you don't even need a Band-Aid."

"*Pledge*," I said. "I pledge to always try to do the right thing for my daughter."

"*Pledge*," Anastasia said. The purple feathers of her pen danced as she wrote. "I pledge allegiance to the flag of the United States of America."

"*Jungle*," I said. "It's a jungle out there."

"*Jungle*," Anastasia said. "I want to go to a jungle to see the monkeys and orangutans."

"*Surprise*," I said. "When you least expect it, life can sometimes bring a big surprise."

"*Surprise*," Anastasia said. She took her time, forming each letter carefully in her big, loopy script. "Kids always love a big surprise."

This list was killing me. What were these fourth grade spelling book people thinking?

I took a deep breath. "*Plate*," I said. "When company comes, you set an extra plate."

"*Plate*," my sweet, innocent, vulnerable little daughter said, her fluffy pen poised over the sheet of lined white paper.

I couldn't take it anymore. I put my hand over hers. "Honey . . ."

"Wait," she said. She shook off my hand and started writing. "When I have my own house, everyone who visits will get their own pink plate."

"Honey," I said again.

She finally looked up. When she saw my face, she tilted her head.

"Guess what?" I said, trying to make my voice both casual and reassuring. It sounded totally phony, even to me.

She narrowed her eyes. *"What?"*

The words felt stuck in my throat. I pushed them out. "Your dad called. He wants to see you."

Her face lit up instantly, brilliantly, the way a flick of the switch lights up a cold, dark hallway.

"*My* dad?" she said.

I nodded.

"My *dad*?" she said.

I nodded again.

Anastasia's pink and purple pen belly-flopped to the table. "Come on, *hurry*. I want to see my dad. *Now*."

When I'd rehearsed this conversation in my head, it had gone a lot differently. I'd pictured us sitting next to each other on the couch, the way we would have in a sitcom. I'd put my arm around my daughter and say just the right thing. She'd say just the right thing back. Then we'd cut to a commercial.

I reached for something worthy of the enormity of the situation, but it felt like my brain was packed in Styrofoam. "Um," I said. "Not tonight. Sunday. He's coming here Sunday. For a visit."

Anastasia jumped out of her chair. "*Now*. I need to talk to him right now."

"Honey," I said. "It's already all set up for Sunday."

She put her hands on her hips. "On the phone then. Call him."

"Sweetie, I can't. It's only . . ."

"Fine," she said. "Then I'll call him."

We stared each other down. I looked away first.

"Fine," I said. I unplugged the headphone from my cell phone. I found the number of the last call. Technically, I was still working, but any GGG calls that came in would go through to voice mail, and I could always call back.

I looked up. Anastasia's hand was out. She was tapping her foot.

I pushed Call and handed her the phone.

"Daddy?" she said a moment later. Her voice was calm, confident. "Daddy, it's your daughter, Anastasia." She waved me away with her nontelephone hand.

Tears blinded my eyes, and I turned my head quickly so she wouldn't see them. It was a good thing I knew my way to the bathroom by heart, because I might not have found it otherwise.

I put the lid down and sat on the toilet seat. I sobbed quietly, rocking back and forth, my hands crossed over my chest and wrapped around me like the hug I needed. If I'd had to take a test to define the emotions I was feeling, I would have failed miserably. I felt sad, mad, glad, bad—maybe all of Anastasia's short *a* spelling words rolled into one big muddy mess. Mostly, I wanted to crawl under my covers and stay there.

I forced myself to blow my nose and get up. I managed to avoid my image in the mirror while I splashed cold water on my face. I listened at the bathroom door for the sound of Anastasia's voice, but I couldn't hear anything.

I tiptoed into the living room. Anastasia was sitting on the couch, flipping through the album of photos of Seth.

"Hey," I whispered. "How did it go?"

She smiled up at me. "We're having a welcome home party. I'm going to make the decorations, and Dad's going to bring the presents. What do you want to do?"

I looked at her. I twisted my mouth into a smile.

Scream, I thought. While the daughter and the father plan their reunion, what the mother wants to do is scream.

11

NOT THAT I WAS AN EXPERT, BUT IT SEEMED TO ME THAT my best bet for removing the rusty metal railings was to chip away at the cement that anchored the posts to the ground.

I wasn't exactly the kind of person who got all domestic under stress. But I'd been awake for hours, straightening up my bedroom/office and cleaning the bathroom. I'd even started washing the windows. My plan was that I'd keep picking away on the insides of the windows, then move on to the outsides, so they'd all be spotless by Sunday.

Maybe it was my way of staying anchored to my house, when everything in me wanted to grab Anastasia and run. My brain knew I wouldn't do it, but my body wasn't cooperating. I was wired with nervous energy and truly understood the expression *jumping out of my skin*. I was ready to jump out of my skin *and* my life.

I slid the flat end of the screwdriver into a crack in the cement. I couldn't care less what Seth thought of my housekeeping, or anything else, for that matter. But a part of me wanted him to see firsthand that even though he'd stacked the deck against me, I'd managed not only to carry on, but to make everything I touched sparkle, literally as well as figuratively. Anastasia might need occasional, evenly spaced visits from him—what child wouldn't—but, even though he owed me—big time—I didn't *need* a thing from him.

I hit the other end of the screwdriver with the hammer. Nothing. I tried wiggling it back and forth. Still nothing. I stepped back and gave the metal railing a whack with the hammer.

It let out a loud bell-like ring. The kids at the bus stop all turned in my direction. Anastasia shook her head to let me know that I was the most embarrassing mother ever.

"Sorry," I mouthed.

The bus rolled down the street and stopped. I watched Anastasia fall into line with the other kids, climb the steps, and disappear from view. She didn't reappear, which meant she'd chosen a seat on the side of the bus I couldn't see.

The bus driver beeped.

Cynthia's three kids came running out of their house. Lexi was combing her hair with a wide-tooth comb. Treasure was still zipping up her backpack. Parker took a final bite of his Pop-Tart and threw the wrapper over his shoulder as he ran.

Cynthia jogged down the sidewalk behind them. She was wearing a baby blue tank top and a matching tennis skirt. "I saw that," she yelled. "Get back here right now and pick that up, young man."

Parker half turned around.

The bus driver gunned the motor.

"Parker," Cynthia yelled. "You know how I feel about re-membering what planet we're on."

I sprinted over and picked up the Pop-Tart wrapper. "Got it," I yelled.

Parker climbed up the stairs of the bus. The doors barely cleared his backside when they closed.

"Say thank you to Miss Murray," Cynthia yelled after the bus, though I noticed she made no effort to collect Parker's Pop-Tart wrapper.

She turned to me. "Is it Ms. Murray or Miss Murray? I never know what to tell my kids to call people when they don't have a husband."

"Actually," I said, "I seem to have one again. At least technically."

It wasn't so much that I'd decided to confide in Cynthia when I said it. It was more like trying out the sound of something in an empty auditorium.

"Where is he?" she said. She squinted in the direction of my house, as if she'd need a husband sighting before she believed me.

I laughed. "He's not here." I gave the railing another whack with the hammer.

Cynthia put her hands over her ears. "Oh, you're so lucky. Make-up sex is just the best."

"No, no, no," I said, even though her hands were still over her ears. "It's not like that."

Cynthia kept her hands on her ears but separated her fingers. "Oh, give it a chance. It definitely is. When Decker and I have just finished fighting, the sex is almost perfect."

"*Almost* perfect?" I smiled. "Isn't that an oxymoron?"

Cynthia smiled back. "Sometimes. But he's my oxymoron."

I wondered if it would be worth rewinding to the part where Cynthia first walked out her door, so that we could start all over again. "Hey," I said. "Remember those power tools you mentioned? Do you think I could borrow one, maybe a chain saw or something?"

"Oh, right," Cynthia said. She walked away.

I hit the railing again. Then I traded the hammer for the screwdriver. I squatted down, stabbed the screwdriver into another crack at the base of a different post, and wiggled the handle around and around. Eventually I managed to release a tiny sprinkle of cement dust. At this rate, I'd have one of the two railings down by Thanksgiving. The good news was I was starting to sweat—who knew that demolition was such good exercise. No wonder you never saw carpenters jogging down the street.

I stood up. Cynthia was walking my way, one hand swinging a big silver and pink case. It looked like a heftier version of the Barbie briefcase Anastasia had talked me into buying her a few years ago.

"Here you go," Cynthia said.

It was surprisingly heavy. "Thanks," I said. "I'll return it as soon as I finish."

"No rush," she said. "I never use it. I just take it with me when I'm trying to get a job."

No wonder she'd only had one client since she'd moved here.

She turned and started walking away. "If I'm not back in time for the bus . . . ," she said over her shoulder.

"Got it," I said.

I sat down on my front steps and snapped open the case's two silver locks. The tools were all the pinkest of pink: a pink hammer, a pink box of nails, pink wrenches, pink pliers, a pink level, two rolls of pink duct tape in different widths, pink gloves, even a pink bandanna and pink safety goggles. For contrast, the case was lined in black velvet, and each item had its own home behind a loop of pink elastic.

It was both brilliant and a little bit scary.

I'd been hoping for a miniature pink chain saw, but no such luck. Maybe it was actually a good thing, since I wasn't sure I'd have the guts to use a chain saw anyway, even a pink one.

The closest thing I could find was a small hand saw with a pink handle and cute little teeth. I slid it out from its slot in the case and sat down cross-legged on the walkway. I positioned the blade on one of the posts, as close to the ground as I could get it, and started sawing away.

The tiny pink saw was amazing. It bit right into the rusty metal. I sawed back and forth, and back and forth, building up speed, feeling the burn of unused muscles in my arms and back. I imagined the old railing down, the new one up, my house looking like a page from *Coastal Living* magazine, all by the time Anastasia stepped off the bus.

A little ways into the post, the resistance got tougher. I moved onto my hands and knees so I could put my whole body into my sawing. I was working up a good sweat now. No wonder people got into the home improvement thing. Maybe I could look into a free class at Home Depot. Maybe Anastasia could take it with me.

Exactly midway through the post, the saw got stuck. I tried pushing. Then I tried pulling. I tried pushing some more. It didn't budge. I tried to wiggle the saw free. It stayed stuck.

I rooted through Cynthia's silver and pink case, section by section, looking for something, anything.

Finally I went into the house and started going through my cupboards. There weren't a lot of options, so I settled for a can of Pam. I headed back outside. To save time, I shook the can of cooking spray vigorously for the recommended sixty seconds as I walked. I sprayed the saw and the post carefully, making sure I avoided the saw's pink handle, so it didn't get slippery.

I put the Pam down and grabbed the saw by the handle.

The saw started to move again, smooth as butter. Or at least Pam. "Ah, the indefatigable ingenuity of the pinker sex," I said out loud.

Apparently I spoke too soon. One saw forward and half a saw back, and the saw and I were stuck again. I pushed. I pulled. I switched angles. I wiggled. I sprayed the rest of the can of Pam on it.

I took a step back. A few inches above ground level, Cynthia's little pink saw stuck out of my rusty metal post like a tomahawk. It would be the first thing Seth saw when he climbed the steps on Sunday, a huge pink flag that I wasn't even close to having it together after all.

I grabbed the pink-handled hammer again. I put on the pink safety glasses. I swung back the full length of my arm and let my stupid metal railing have it with all my might.

I kept swinging and swinging. Somewhere along the line I realized I was swinging at Seth, too, for leaving me, but also for waltzing back into our lives, not when I needed him, but when *he* felt like it. Once again he was calling the shots, giving me no choice but to deal with it, with him, whether I wanted to or not.

By the time I stopped, I was dripping with sweat and pieces of rusted metal scrollwork were scattered everywhere. Cynthia's little pink saw still hadn't budged an inch.

I walked out to the sidewalk to survey my progress. My front walkway looked like a metal sculpture garden gone bad. Or maybe a stop on a metal recycling plant tour. I wondered if it would look better or worse if I dragged the new porch railings over and propped them up against the ones I'd managed to take from awful to awfuller. Maybe I could at least get a few points if I could show *intent*.

I gave up and put the rest of Cynthia's pink tools away, before I ruined those, too. Once again, I'd made a complete mess of things.

Really, it was the story of my life. I'd messed up my marriage, my life, my daughter's life. When Seth came to visit on

Sunday, I'd say the wrong things and mess up our lives some more. He'd run away again, and with my luck, it wouldn't be long before Anastasia was right behind him.

Everything I touched turned to rust, and there wasn't a pink tool kit in the world that could save me.

12

"ALOHA," A WOMAN'S VOICE SAID AFTER I FINISHED MY GGG spiel.

"Aloha," I responded.

"No, no, it's a question. Can you tell me if it's true that *aloha* means both 'hello' and 'good-bye'?"

"It does indeed," I said. "And it can also mean 'I love you.'"

"Really? But, what if you meet some guy in Hawaii and you think he's saying I love you, and he's really telling you good-bye. I mean, doesn't that get confusing?"

I looked over at the clock on my living room wall. I pictured the pointy arms circling around and around in slow motion until today's endless shift was over. I couldn't believe this was my life.

I flopped across the couch and put my feet up on the old trunk that served as a coffee table. "Not really," I said. "You just have to pay attention to the tone of voice and the context."

What I was really thinking was that if you couldn't tell if the guy you were with was about to say I love you or good-bye, you should probably find another guy. But who was I to give advice about love in any language.

I took a deep breath. "It's part of the beauty of the Hawaiian culture. *Aloha* is a way of showing affection, compassion, and kindness—essentially the elements that make up the culture of the Hawaiian Islands. It's a very accepting, inclusive place, partly because there are so many influences and ethnicities—Chinese,

Filipino, Japanese, Korean, Portuguese, Samoan, Puerto Rican, Vietnamese, Thai. Hawaii is a great reminder that the world is a melting pot, and we're all pretty much a bunch of mutts."

A call beeped in. "Excuse me," I said. "Let me just put another call on hold. I'll be right back."

I clicked the Call button. "Great Girlfriend Geta—"

"Hi, it's Joni."

"Oh, hi," I said. "Listen, I've got a potential group on the line. I'll call you right back, okay?"

"Can you stop by the office when you get a chance?"

I looked at the clock. If I left now and didn't stay for more than an hour, I could make it back for the bus.

"Sure," I said. "I'll be right there."

I clicked back to the other call and picked up the pace. "We have two GGG trips to the Hawaiian islands, one to the big island and one to Maui. Would you like me to see that you get some information?"

"Can we all take hula lessons?"

"Absolutely," I said. "They're actually included in both tours. You've just missed the Merrie Monarch Festival, which is Hawaii's biggest hula competition, but you can still get there in time for Lei Day."

"Ooh, that sounds good."

"Doesn't it?" I admitted.

I sighed. I took a final gulp of my tea and walked the cup over to my kitchen sink. "Oh, and you *have* to take the side trip to the Kilauea Volcano. Legend has it Madame Pele, the powerful volcano goddess, makes her home in the Halemaunau firepit there. But be careful, if you try to take a souvenir rock from her volcano, she'll hunt you down and plague you forever with bad luck."

"Sounds like my sister-in-law. But it's kind of a family reunion, so we have to take her with us."

"Well," I said. "I'm sure you'll have a good time anyway."

I took down her mailing info. "Okay. I guess that's aloha then."

"Aloha." She giggled. "And I totally get which kind."

"My work here is done," I said.

JONI WAS SITTING in the middle of the floor surrounded by cartons of paperwork.

I opened the glass door, and she looked up at the sound of the bell.

"Aloha," I said.

Joni smiled. "Aloha yourself." She shook her head. "Geez Loueez, how could I let things pile up like this?"

"Easy to do," I said as I leaned over to give her a kiss on the top of her head. "Here, let me help."

"There isn't enough help in the world."

Something in her voice got my attention.

"Are you okay?" I said.

"Sit," she said.

I slid a cardboard carton out of the way and sat down on the floor across from her. She was wearing jeans and a long-sleeved gray T-shirt that exactly matched her hair.

"I'm thinking about selling," she said.

"The company?"

Joni rubbed her scalp with the fingers of both hands. "If I can even find a buyer in this economy. I'd probably be lucky to give it away right now."

"You can't sell," I said.

She smiled. "You'll be fine. Anastasia's getting older. It wouldn't hurt you to find a job where you had to leave the house."

"I leave the house," I said. "I'm here, aren't I?"

Joni leaned over and put her hands on my knees. "Jill. Honey. I'm old and tired, and you're young and stuck. It's time."

We looked at each other. I tried to think of something positive to say, maybe wish her well, thank her for all the years she'd been there for me, ask her what she was planning to do with all her free time once she sold. Tai chi on the beach? That Photoshop class she could never fit in?

"But, what am I going to do?" was all that came out of my mouth. I bit down on my lower lip so I wouldn't cry.

As soon as Joni wrapped her arms around my shoulders, I started to sob. She patted my back, rocking me back and forth the way I'd rocked Anastasia a thousand times.

"It'll be fine," she said. "Nothing's going to happen right away."

I lifted my head off her shoulder and looked around for a tissue.

"Desk," Joni said. "Back right corner."

After I finished blowing my nose, I sat on the edge of Joni's desk. I was still rocking, I noticed.

"What if I started doing more work?" I said. "You know, take most of the load off your shoulders? Or maybe you could scale things back, just keep the trips that are consistently filling up. I could put together a list of recommendations for you. . . ."

Joni pushed herself up off the floor. "I think the best thing for me would be a clean break. But don't worry, when and if I find a new owner, there'll be plenty of time for us to get in there and pitch you and your ideas, if you decide that's what you want to do."

"Seth is back," I said, as if it might somehow make a difference, as if for some crazy reason Joni might say, *Oh, Seth is back? Well, of course, now that I know that, I wouldn't even consider selling. It would be far too much stress for you to have to deal with both at once.*

Joni shook her head. "Men. You can't even count on them to run away reliably."

"Ha," I said.

Joni's watery blue eyes held mine. "How's it going?"

I rocked back and forth while I thought about it. "I don't know. I mean, I know how much having a dad in her life would mean to Anastasia, but I'm just not sure I can get past wanting to kill him for what he did to us. All those years of nothing. No letters, no phone calls. No money."

"How long has it been now?"

I shook my head and reached for another tissue. "Seven years. And now he thinks he can waltz right back into our lives, all good intentions, like he's never been gone."

"Well, you'd certainly be within your rights to kill him, but it's messy, and the cops always go after the deserted wives first." Joni opened the little office refrigerator. She took out two bottled waters and handed me one. "So maybe your best bet is to let him waltz. Just make sure you lead."

"Thanks." I opened my water and took a long, parched gulp. "But what if he does it again? I mean, Anastasia would be devastated."

Joni took a sip and screwed the top back on her bottle. "You can't control that. If he takes off again, you and Anastasia will be there for each other, just like you were the first time around."

I guzzled some more water. "And the other thing is the money. I mean, how do I get past that? Do you know what I could do with seven years of child support?"

Joni smiled. "Buy me out?"

"Exactly," I said, even though I wasn't completely sure that would be the way I'd go. Somewhere behind a towering mountain of anxiety, a whisper of a voice was telling me maybe Joni was right—I was stuck, and it was time to move on to something else. With seven years of child support I'd have the incredible luxury of shifting out of survival mode and getting to a place where I could actually think about what I *wanted* to do.

"Let it go," Joni said.

"Let it go?" I repeated.

Joni nodded. "And I quote: 'At the end of every seven years you shall grant a release of debts.' "

"That's ridiculous. Where did you even get that?"

Joni grinned. "The Internet, of course. Where does everybody get everything these days? But it's from the Bible—Deuteronomy, I think. The next part goes something like, 'Every creditor who has lent anything to his neighbor shall release it. . . .' "

"I don't think it applies to this situation. Seth wasn't a neighbor." I slid off the edge of Joni's desk and walked over to look out the window. "He was a husband and a father. Is. Was. Whatever."

Joni waited until I turned around. "It's not about him," she said.

"What do you mean?"

"It's about you. Honey, if you don't forgive him, it'll eat you alive."

13

NOW I KNEW WHY JAMES TAYLOR WROTE THAT SONG about going to Carolina in his mind. I was trying to stay calm by going to Hawaii in mine, while I sat cross-legged on the floor of my imaginary lanai overlooking the ocean. Over the years, Anastasia and I had made leis with everything from hyacinths to dandelions, but I'd always dreamed of the incredible extravagance of using fresh orchids. So that's what I was pretending to do.

It takes fifty orchid blossoms to make each single-strand lei. I was using imaginary pinkish purple and white dendrobium orchids, which are not only beautiful, but also resilient and long-lived. In fact, if I could *be* an orchid, I'd probably want to be a pinkish purple and white dendrobium.

And if I could be anywhere, it would be anywhere but here. I pushed myself off the floor of my ordinary bedroom. I closed my closet door and tried to slow my breathing. I resisted the urge to climb back into bed and pull the covers over my head.

I willed myself back to Hawaii. The *kui* method of lei making involves stringing the flowers together by passing a long needle and thread through the center of each flower. There's also a braiding method called *haku*, which includes ti leaves, the same leaves used to make hula skirts, as well as a twining method called *wili*. I decided to go with the *kui*.

If I were planning one of GGG's Hawaii trips, our first activity would be to take a lei-making class. The act of creating beauty through repetitive motion was soothing, calming, a zen experience really. It might well end up being the highlight of our entire trip.

I stood up again. Before I thought to look away, I caught myself in the mirror over my dresser. "So much for the zen of imaginary lei making," I whispered to my worried face.

"Aloha," Anastasia said when I walked into the living room. She was wearing her grass skirt, part of her Halloween costume from last year, over a pink leotard and tights. Her pink headband held a faux silk orchid in place behind one ear. The orange flower made her hazel eyes look almost jade green. Her long dark hair was freshly washed and shiny.

She took my breath away.

"Aloha," I said.

Anastasia looked up from the poster she was coloring and wrinkled her nose. "Change your clothes, okay, Mom?"

I looked down at my favorite jeans. "Why?"

"Mom, it's a *luau*."

It wasn't worth fighting about, so I traded the jeans for a funky old flowered skirt that had kind of an island feel, if you didn't get too literal about it. The Hawaiian theme for Seth's welcome home party had been my idea. I thought "aloha" would be a good operating principle, since the way I saw it, this hello was still essentially a good-bye, and I'd need all the compassion and kindness I could muster just to get through it.

The fact that I was getting a jump start on my prep for tomorrow's Lunch Around the World class made me feel a little bit better about actually cooking for a man I would probably just as soon feed rat poison. But what could I do? Anastasia was only ten. It wasn't as if I could hand her the car keys and wish her happy shopping.

I walked back into the living room and executed an exaggerated model's turn on bare feet. My skirt circled out around me. "Better?" I asked.

Anastasia looked me up and down, every inch the ten-year-old critic. "A little makeup might help," she said finally.

I ignored her. I was trying my hardest not to ruin this day for Anastasia. Sharing her excitement was beyond me, but I was hoping I was a good enough mother that I could at least be a blank slate for her happiness to bounce off. I'd contribute a little cleaning and cooking to the cause. And while I was dying to take off to Hawaii for real the minute Seth showed up, I'd force myself to stay, to be there for my daughter, to make sure Seth didn't screw things up.

Anastasia had been practically airborne since she'd talked to Seth. She'd spent her time before and after school twirling through the house, her long hair whipping around behind her. She hopped ten times on one foot, ten on the other, then nine and nine, eight and eight, working her way down to one, then back up to ten again. She went out to our postage stamp backyard and turned cartwheel after cartwheel after cartwheel.

And the whole time I kept thinking: *If he breaks her heart, I'll kill him.*

Anastasia held up the poster she'd made. It was covered with red hearts and pink daisies. WELCOME HOME DADDY floated across the top in purple balloon letters, and under that a smiling trio of hula dancers held hands. I looked a little closer. Mama hula dancer, papa hula dancer, and baby daughter hula dancer smiled back at me.

"Good job, honey," I said, hoping my voice didn't sound quite as strangled as it felt.

I helped Anastasia tape up her poster over the fireplace, and then we put on the *Drew's Famous Hawaiian Luau Party Music* CD Anastasia had picked out at the library. I'd wanted something a little bit more authentic and less like Hawaiian elevator music, but Anastasia's choice in music turned out to be the perfect touch. How stressed could you be while you were listening to the theme music from *Hawaii Five-0*?

Anastasia and I had found fresh pineapples on sale, so we bought two—one for today and one for my class tomorrow. I started peeling and cutting up both of them, while she threaded the big chunks of juicy pineapple onto wooden skewers.

We moved on to making Huli Huli Chicken to the beat of "Surfin' USA," taking a little break to dance around the kitchen—doing the swim, of course. Every couple of strokes we'd hold our nose and bend our knees and pretend to go under water.

We mixed chicken broth, frozen pineapple juice concentrate, soy sauce, ketchup, Worcestershire sauce, and chopped ginger in our biggest Pyrex mixing bowl. It wasn't a fussy recipe—nothing from Hawaii was ever fussy—so I just guessed on the amounts.

We soaked some more bamboo skewers in water, which would keep them from burning when the chicken cooked. I opened the jumbo packs of boneless chicken thighs, trimmed off the fat, and cut them into bite-size pieces, then plopped them into the marinade. Anastasia covered the bowl with plastic wrap and put it in the refrigerator while I washed my hands.

Anastasia and I had been preparing food together since she was old enough to stand up on a chair beside me at the kitchen counter, so we had a nice, easy rhythm. "Kokomo" was playing now, and we sang along, faking the words until we got back to the Aruba, Jamaica part.

"We have to remember to show my dad all my old report cards," Anastasia said when "Kokomo" was over. "He'll like me better if he knows I'm smart."

I was holding a clear glass lemonade pitcher that had belonged to my mother. I put it down carefully on the speckled Formica counter.

"Sweetie . . . ," I said.

Anastasia slid the pitcher closer to her and started pouring in the lime juice. "But we should show him pictures first, especially the ones when my soccer team made it to the play-offs."

I opened the pineapple juice concentrate slowly. "You don't have to prove anything to him . . . ," I said, casually, conversationally, as if my stomach hadn't just tied itself into a million knots at the realization that my daughter saw today as a *tryout*. If she did well, Seth would be back in her life. If not, then he'd just go looking for a smarter girl, one who played better soccer, somewhere else.

Anastasia took the opened can from my hand. She was looking straight ahead, as if she didn't have a care in the world and didn't even know I was in the room with her, but I could tell she was waiting for me to finish my sentence, to tell her why she didn't have to prove anything to the father she hadn't seen for seven years.

I wanted to say, *Of course he'll stay in your life. You're brilliant, sweet, and funny. You're so incredibly beautiful, inside and out. How could he possibly resist you?*

But the truth sat on the counter between us like a big fat white elephant. Whatever the missing secret ingredient, somehow the recipe that included Anastasia and me hadn't been enough once before.

"The Tide Is High" was playing now. The perky line about wanting to be your number one was making me wonder if there was a DJ in the sky somewhere with a twisted sense of humor.

I handed Anastasia a big wooden spoon to stir the Luau Punch. "When your dad left," I said, "it wasn't about you. You are the best thing that ever happened to either of us. Nothing about you could be more perfect—you're smart, you're kind, you're talented, you're pretty, you're loveable. And you're loved. Whatever happens, I will always love you."

The sound of three distinct, evenly spaced knocks came into the kitchen like punctuation. Randomly, I thought of that old song about knocking three times on the ceiling if you want me. I hoped Drew had had the good sense not to include it on this CD.

"He's here!" Anastasia yelled. She dropped the wooden spoon and ran.

Just as she opened the front door, the song changed again. *Don't Worry, Be Happy.*

14

"HEY. YOU MUST BE ASIA."

"Hey. You must be my dad."

My eyes teared up, even though I'd sworn I wouldn't let them. I wanted to float up to the ceiling, numb, ethereal. I could be Anastasia's guardian angel, keeping an eye on her but not feeling the pain of this world.

They stood like that for a long moment—the door wide open, Seth with one foot on the threshold, the other still outside on the cracked cement step. I had this sudden awful feeling he might turn and run. I wanted to run. All those years they'd been apart stretched between them, almost visible, like a long winding trail of loss.

Finally, Seth pulled the front door closed behind him.

Anastasia held out a lei with both hands. It was royal blue and made out of crinkly plastic.

Seth leaned down. She looped it over his head.

"Aloha," Anastasia said.

"Aloha," Seth said.

There was a long, awkward moment.

"You can hug me if you want to," Anastasia said.

"Thank you," Seth said.

He set the shopping bag he was carrying down on the floor. He leaned forward and put his arms out, carefully.

Anastasia threw her arms around his neck.

Seth stood up straight and lifted Anastasia off the floor. He wrapped his arms around her and twisted back and forth. Her hula skirt made a rustling sound as her legs swung from side to side.

His eyes met mine over her head. They were shiny with tears.

I looked away.

Seth choked back a sob. Anastasia patted him on his back as if she were burping a baby. "It's okay, Dad," she said.

"I can do cartwheels," Anastasia announced the second her feet touched the ground again.

"When you were little, I used to hold your feet so you could walk on your hands," Seth said.

"Cartwheels are much harder," Anastasia said. "Want me to show you?"

"Sure," Seth said. He wiped his eyes with the back of one hand. Anastasia grabbed his other hand and pulled him toward the kitchen door. If we were still married, I would have gotten him a tissue, I thought randomly.

After the door slammed, I just stood there. The shopping bag Seth had brought with him was still sitting on the floor. I certainly wasn't going to pick it up.

The music changed to a tinny version of "Wipeout."

I followed the sound, happy that I could turn off at least some of the noise in my head.

WHEN ANASTASIA AND SETH finally came in, they were laughing. They both had beads of sweat mixed with the freckles on their noses, and their ears were an identical shade of red. Seth's shirt was all wrinkled from rolling around in the yard, and he had a dandelion stuck behind one ear. He was still wearing his blue plastic lei. Anastasia had grass stains on the knees of both pink tights. I'd probably never get them out.

I felt a piercing stab of jealousy.

I grabbed a book of matches and headed for the back door to light our little Weber minigrill.

Seth held out his hand. "I'll get that," he said.

"No thanks," I said. "I've pretty much got it down by now."

When I came back inside, Seth was helping Anastasia set the table. It was the right thing to do, but it still pissed me off. *How dare you touch our silverware?* I wanted to yell. *How dare you touch our plates and our paper napkins? How dare you come anywhere near us after all this time?*

I dug deep, trying to feel happy for Anastasia that she appeared to be having a healthy, if seriously overdue, bonding experience with her father, at the same time I focused on staying detached enough to ignore said father.

I attempted a deep breath, but even this turned out to be more difficult than it should have been. Maybe keeping my heart shut down made it harder for my other vital organs to function. The air seemed somehow thicker since Seth had arrived, almost liquid, and my body seemed to be telling me that if I breathed in too much at once, my lungs would fill up and I'd drown. My breathing stayed shallow, almost like panting.

I started threading the chunks of chicken onto wet wooden skewers. Anastasia opened the refrigerator and put the platter of pineapple kabobs on the table. She poured a bag of baby carrots into a little bowl and placed them next to the pineapple.

Seth reached for the refrigerator door.

"Excuse me?" I said.

"Just trying to help," he said.

We looked at each other.

"Or not," he said. He walked over and took a seat at our tiny kitchen table.

"Want some Hawaiian punch, Daddy?" Anastasia said.

How about a nice Hawaiian Punch? a voice from the old commercial said into my ear. If I were Punchy, the Hawaiian Punch mascot, as soon as Seth said yes, I could haul back and deck him. I couldn't imagine anything feeling much better right now.

"Thanks, Asia," Seth said. "I'd love some punch."

"She goes by Anastasia," I said.

"That's only because you never told me about Asia," Anastasia said. "Mom, can you go put some more music on?"

"Did something happen to your feet?" I asked sweetly.

Anastasia turned to Seth. "She gets like this sometimes. Don't worry, she'll calm down."

He laughed. He stopped as soon as he saw my face and started to stand up.

"I'll get it," I said.

As soon as I pushed Play, and Keali'i Reichel's lush music floated through the house, I felt better. I carefully inhaled and exhaled a few cleansing breaths. "You're almost there," I whispered to myself.

"Nice music," Seth said as I walked back into the kitchen. He retrieved his shopping bag and pulled out a bottle of red wine. "In lieu of Luau Punch?"

I weighed the chance to say something mean against the fact that I couldn't remember the last time I'd had a glass of wine.

"Okay," I said.

"Am I allowed to look for glasses and a corkscrew?" he said.

Anastasia watched our every move, as if she were at the zoo and we were the exotic animals she'd come to see.

"Whatever," I said.

"Great," he said. "But first . . ." He pulled out a wooden box and put it on the table in front of Anastasia.

Her eyes lit up. She ran her hand across the top of the dark, intricately carved box reverently. "Thank you," she said. "It's just what I've always wanted."

Seth burst out laughing. "Don't worry. There's stuff inside."

Anastasia opened the box. It was filled with small cloth dolls. They were all about the same size, maybe six inches tall or so. Each one was female and completely unique. Their skin tones ranged from cappuccino to espresso, and a bold array of bright geometric print fabrics was wrapped around their bodies and knotted on top of their heads.

Anastasia slid her plate back. She took them out of the box carefully, laying them side by side across the table.

"You're probably too old for dolls now . . . ," Seth said.

"Not this kind," she said.

"They're handmade Senegalese pocket dolls," Seth said. "One of the things I did in West Africa was to help build partnerships between local artisans and fair trade organizations in the United States and Canada."

"I love them," Anastasia said.

I turned away to check on the rice. I grabbed the chicken off the counter.

Seth looked up at me. "And this is for you, Jill. . . ."

I ignored him and walked out to the grill. I stood there while the skewers of chicken cooked, taking big deep gasps of air, not even caring that I was probably inhaling smoke and Huli Huli Chicken grease.

I'd just finished turning the chicken, when the kitchen door opened and Seth came out. He was holding two glasses of red wine.

He reached one out to me.

"Just leave it on the table in the kitchen," I said. "I'll get it when I have time."

Seth took a sip from one of the glasses.

I moved the chicken skewers around some more on the grill, just for something to do.

"Look," Seth said. "I know this can't be easy for you."

I spun around fast enough to make myself dizzy. "*Look*," I said. "You don't know anything about me, so don't kid yourself. You don't know who I am, how I've changed, what I've been through. You don't have any idea what I'm feeling or not feeling."

I reached for my wineglass. Seth let it go without a word.

I took a big sip. "And *listen*," I said. "I love my daughter enough to know she needs you in her life, but it has nothing to do with the two of us. So get over yourself, okay?"

He just looked at me. I took another sip, trying to taste the wine, but even my taste buds were numb, and it might as well have been punch. I turned my full attention to the Huli Huli Chicken.

When the door creaked open, we both turned around. A Senegalese pocket doll appeared, followed by most of Anastasia's arm.

The doll danced back and forth like a puppet.

"Aloha," it said in Anastasia's voice.

15

DREW'S FAMOUS HAWAIIAN LUAU PARTY MUSIC WAS cranked all the way up on the cheap plastic CD player in the community center kitchen. My Lunch Around the World class had spontaneously formed a conga line and was dancing around the kitchen in their crinkly plastic leis.

Conga lines originated in Cuba and later became popular as Latin American *carnaval* marches. It wasn't until the 1930s that they made their way into the United States. It was a stretch to connect them culturally to Hawaii in any way. It was even more of a stretch to make the one-two-three-kick pattern of the steps work with the beat of "Wipeout." But if it didn't bother the class, I certainly wasn't going to worry about it. I yawned and stretched discreetly, then went back to threading the now extremely well-marinated Huli Huli Chicken onto bamboo skewers.

After Seth left last night, it was hard to know just what to say to Anastasia. Especially since she went right to her room and shut the door. I tiptoed up and down the little hallway a few times, pausing to listen casually outside her bedroom door. On one trip by, I thought I heard her talking to her stuffed animals, or maybe to the Senegalese pocket dolls.

I walked into the kitchen. I opened the jar of shea butter, a soothing cream made from a nut that grows wild in West Africa, and rubbed some on my hands. Just because it came from Seth didn't mean I couldn't use it.

Eventually, I walked back to Anastasia's room and knocked. "Time to brush your teeth and go to beh-ed," I called, sounding like a bad imitation of somebody trying to be a good mother.

Anastasia opened her door, carrying her pink nightgown. She walked by me as if I were invisible.

I knocked on the bathroom door. "Make sure you give me the tights so I can get those grass stains out," I said.

The door opened a second later, and Anastasia's tights landed at my feet.

"Thanks," I said to the closed door.

When Anastasia came out, I was still standing there holding her tights.

"What?" she said.

"Nothing," I said. "I was just going to come into your room and talk to you for a minute."

She walked by me without a word.

I followed her into her room. I pictured her climbing into bed, and me tucking her in and smoothing out the covers. Then I'd sit on the edge of her bed. We'd go over every detail of Seth's visit, sharing her highest hopes and my deepest fears.

She stopped just inside the door and crossed her arms over her chest.

"What?" she said.

I leaned back against the doorframe casually.

"So," I said. "How did it go with your dad?"

She squinted up at me. "You were there," she said.

"Good point," I said. "Well, I think it went great. You two really seemed to hit it off."

"Can I go to bed now?" she said.

"Sure, honey. You must be tired after all that." I took a moment to fake a yawn. "Wow, me, too." I leaned over to give her a kiss. "Okay, good night, Anastasia."

She looked me right in the eyes. "It's Asia," she said. "From now on it's Asia."

Okay, so from now on it would be Asia, and maybe in another seven years I'd be able to call her that without triggering a flashback to our early years as a family. I plunged a skewer into a piece of chicken and pretended it was Seth.

By the time I finished threading the chicken onto the skewers, Seth was riddled with holes and I was feeling a bit more chipper. I arranged them on the community center's well-used cookie sheets, which Ethel and her friends had wrapped in foil while T-shirt Tom preheated the oven. I'd planned on bringing my little Weber grill with me today and setting it out on the grass next to the building, but this morning when I got up, it just seemed like way too much work.

After Anastasia went to bed, I sat on the couch. Then I got up and poured another half glass of red wine. I sat on the couch some more while I drank the wine. I knew everything would be different after tonight. Even if Seth was already running away—back to Africa or toward some new horizon—the balance of our lives had changed and nothing would ever be the same for Anastasia or me.

Finally I cried. I cried hard. I cried for a family that had once been whole and never would be again. I cried for my daughter and all those missed years with her dad she could never get back. I cried for myself and my dashed dream of a perfect little family in a house full of joy. And somewhere along the line I realized I was also crying for the little girl I'd once been, whose mother ignored her and who never knew her father. The sad and lonely child who'd always believed in her heart that better days were up ahead.

When I was sure she'd been asleep long enough, I tiptoed back into Anastasia's room. She was curled up on her side, hugging an armful of Senegalese pocket dolls. Her face was flushed. One leg poked out of a tangle of covers.

I thought about trying to unravel the covers, but I didn't want to risk it. Instead, I reached under her mattress and carefully wriggled out her diary.

I held my breath until I was back in the hallway. I knew I should have waited until she was safely at school. I knew I shouldn't be doing this at all. But I was like a diary junkie who couldn't wait until morning for her next fix. I leaned back against the wall and angled the pages under the ceiling light. It didn't take long to find tonight's entry.

A my name is Asia

Senagleez pocket dolls

In the middle of a luaw

A dad that was worth waiting for

I shook my head to bring myself back to the community center. T-shirt Tom freed himself from the conga line and came over to open the oven for me. Today's shirt said MY WILD OATS HAVE TURNED TO SHREDDED WHEAT.

"Thanks," I said. I slid the cookie sheets of Huli Huli Chicken inside.

When I stood up, he was looking at me through the fingerprints on his glasses. "Why so glum, chum?" he said.

One of his sidekicks broke away from the conga line and came up to stand with us. "Keep an eye on this one," he said. "He can't be trusted around the pretty young ladies."

Ethel came over, too. "Oh, leave her alone, you old coots," she said. The turquoise sweat suit and matching stretchy headband she was wearing really popped against her orange hair. "She already has a boyfriend. Don't you, honey?"

"Okay," I yelled. "Why don't you dance that line over this way, and we'll get the real party started."

"Oh, no," Ethel whispered. "Is it over already?"

BY THE TIME I FINISHED cleaning up after Lunch Around the World, my phone shift for Great Girlfriend Getaways had begun. I just managed to put the leftovers and everything else into the passenger side of my car before the phone rang.

"Hi," a woman said after I finished answering. "Can you tell me if your Costa Rican surfing trip is full yet?"

"There are a few spots left," I said. The truth was, the more the merrier, and no matter how many women signed up, we'd find a way to make it work. "But it's one of our most popular trips, so I wouldn't wait much longer."

"Have you ever been on it?"

"Not yet," I said.

"Why not?"

Because I haven't been anywhere in almost a decade and essentially I have no life didn't seem like the most positive response.

"It's next on my list," I finally said in what I hoped was a believable voice. I didn't tell her it was probably my bucket list, and that statistically I had approximately four decades to go before I kicked it.

I shifted the phone to my other ear, so I could put the key in the ignition.

"Oh, good," the woman said. "Maybe I'll see you there."

"Absolutely," I lied. "I'll look for you."

Before my shift was over, I'd fed Anastasia leftover Huli Huli Chicken for dinner and answered three more calls about the Costa Rican surfing trip. It was as if the universe was trying to rub it in. I slid my headphone down around my neck, since my ears were starting to get sore.

"Are you almost done with the phone?" Anastasia said. "I told Dad I'd call him after dinner."

"But you just saw him yesterday," I said.

"So," she said.

"First we'll clear the table and load the dishwasher," I said. "And then we'll do your spelling. And then we'll talk."

Anastasia was already halfway over to the dishwasher with our plates. I grabbed the sponge and started wiping off the table.

She drained the last sip of her milk and put the glass in the top rack.

"Done," she said. "Can I have the phone now?"

"Spelling," I said.

She held out her hand. "Dad and I are going to do it over the phone. We already made plans."

16

BILLY SANDERS STOOD UP AND BOWED. I TRIED TO KEEP A dignified look on my face, but I could feel myself grinning from ear to ear at the sight of him. He looked adorably earnest and slightly geeky, the kind of guy I might have hung out with in high school while we both suffered through crushes on cooler, unattainable classmates.

He was wearing black bike shorts and a red T-shirt with the sleeves cut short enough to reveal most of his muscular arms. His helmet was looped over the back of his chair by its strap.

"How do you say *hello* in Japanese?" he asked when he finished bowing.

I reined in my grin and bowed. "The Japanese don't really have a word for *hello*."

"Then what would I say?"

I sat down. I took a moment to smell the cappuccino, then another to savor the sumptuousness of my first sip.

I'd been looking forward to this meeting. Even though I knew it was ridiculous, I'd changed my clothes three times before I left the house today. When I saw her at the bus stop, I even had this crazy urge to ask Cynthia if I could borrow one of her hot little tennis outfits. As if I could pull that off.

I'd started out with yoga pants, which made me look athletic but not very professional. Then I tried on my one good suit, which was relatively flattering, but seemed way too formal for meeting someone who invariably wore bicycle attire. I didn't have a lot of choices in my closet, so I finally settled for my old standby—the Anthropologie skirt and a teal cap-sleeved T-shirt with a V-neck.

I knew time was running out with Billy Sanders. I probably should have cut him loose once I had the business cards made and placed an ad on Craigslist for a go-between to help him out in Japan. Or maybe even stretched it to two more as-yet-unscheduled future sessions—one on the phone once he was in Japan, and one to reassess and talk about his next steps once he returned. Though once he'd found a good go-between, he really shouldn't need me anymore.

But I couldn't quite make myself back away. Instead, I found myself thinking that if I spent some more time learning Japanese, and maybe even researching the bicycle industry, I could make myself legitimately valuable.

Maybe there were even some other countries Billy would want to consider for bicycle rental kiosks before he made a final decision. Bicycles were popular in lots of places besides Japan—Denmark, the Netherlands, Switzerland, Italy, Spain, Germany, France, Belgium, and Australia, just to name a few.

It wasn't that I wanted to take advantage of him, but it was a good gig and it paid well. He was a nice guy, too, and easy to talk to. It would be great to find more ways to work with him.

Last night, as I finished my final sips of wine, I'd fantasized about leaving Anastasia with Seth long enough to go to Japan with Billy as his go-between. Maybe if I could somehow talk him into postponing the trip for a year or two, or even three, I could make it work.

Since Japan was such a traditional culture, and business was still pretty much a man's world over there, ideally the go-between should be male and not female. But I thought the fact that Billy trusted me and knew I'd be looking out for his best interests might make up for any cultural awkwardness my gender presented. And if I had a few years, I could probably learn to speak passable Japanese.

I put my paper cup back down on our table. "You'd greet the person by name, or in this case, you might say good afternoon. That would be Koh-NEE-cheewah."

Billy nodded. "Koh-NEE-cheewah," he said carefully.

"Perfect," I said. Since I hadn't actually started learning more Japanese yet, I took another sip of cappuccino while I searched for something else I could still remember in Japanese. My short stint as a tour guide in Asia was now a distant memory, and we'd had a translator at each stop.

I'd also blocked most of my Japanese memories, since that's where Seth and I had met. Sometimes a picture would come on television, a sky bus in Kyoto or cherry blossoms at Takada Koen Park, and I'd have to close my eyes.

"Koh-NEE-cheewah," Billy said. "Koh-NEE-cheewah, koh-NEE-cheewah."

"Even better," I said. "Okay, now if you want to say, 'My name is Billy Sanders,' you'd say, 'Wah-TAHK-sheewah Billy Sanders.'"

"Wah-TAHK-sheewah Billy Sanders," he said slowly. "Wah-TAHK-sheewah Billy Sanders."

"Great," I said. "Now put them both together." I had no idea if this was something you'd actually do in Japanese, but I'd look it up later.

Billy closed his eyes and concentrated. I watched the way the crinkles at the corners of his eyes crisscrossed the raccoon circles made by his sunglasses.

He opened his eyes and caught me staring. He smiled.

I looked away and took a quick sip of my cappucino.

"Okay," he said. "Koh-NEE-sheewah. Wah-TAHK-cheewah Billy Sanders."

"Close," I said. "But it's Koh-NEE-*chee*wah and Wah-TAHK-*shee*wah."

"Jeez," he said. "They sure don't make it easy, do they?"

I ran a finger around the lip of my coffee cup. "It's a tough language for Americans. But most of the people you'll be discussing business possibilities with will speak English, and as long as they see that you're making an effort, you'll be fine. And your go-between will help you."

Billy leaned forward. "That reminds me," he said. "I think I've found someone."

For a split second, I thought he meant a girlfriend. I could even picture her. She was blond and tan, with long, lean, athletic legs, and expensive streaks in her hair, and she had a whole wardrobe of tennis outfits. Actually, she looked a lot like Cynthia. I had to admit, I didn't really think this woman was Billy's type.

"Wait," I said. "You mean a go-between?"

Billy nodded.

"Great," I said. I supposed in some ways a go-between was better than an incompatible girlfriend, though in other ways it was worse. "But are you sure you shouldn't wait until you get a few more replies so you can compare the candidates?"

He grinned. "It actually wasn't my first response. I also got an invitation to a Japanese love hotel, and an e-mail from someone who claimed to be a certified geisha."

"Gotta love Craigslist," I said.

Billy took the cover off his cappuccino and scooped up the last of the foam with a straw. "But this guy sounds like the real deal."

I felt a little flash of relief at *guy*. "Is he Japanese?"

"He didn't say, but I don't think so. It was definitely an American name. Maybe he's Japanese American." He put the straw down and patted his hip. "I meant to bring his e-mail to show you. . . ." He reached inside his waistband and pulled out a check. "Sorry, I almost forgot this."

Our fingers brushed when he handed it to me. "Thanks," I said. I couldn't believe I'd actually forgotten about the check.

His eyes met mine. "I'm going to meet with him later this week. Do you want to come with me?"

I rummaged in my bag for a notebook and pen. "I think it's probably better if you meet with him yourself, so the relationship is between the two of you. I'll write down a few questions for you though."

"Okay," he said. "How about dinner and a movie sometime then?"

I looked up from my list. "Me?" I said.

He burst out laughing.

I tried to stop myself from blushing, but it only made it worse.

"Sorry," he said. "I didn't mean to laugh. You just looked so surprised. Of course, I meant you."

When I went back to my list, my hand was shaking. I put my pen down and clasped my hands together under the table. "Um," I said. "It's just that I don't really leave my daughter very much. She's still pretty young."

Billy crinkled his eyes. "How old is she?"

"Ten."

He raised an eyebrow. "Well, I guess the good news is in a couple of years you won't have to leave her. She'll leave you."

I heard a big puff of breath escape my lips, like when you blow out air on a frozen winter's day. "I guess maybe that's my plan," I said. I thought I was talking normally, but when it came out, it was barely louder than a whisper.

His raccoon eyes held mine. "Don't you think . . . ," he said.

I could feel my eyes start to tear up.

"Never mind," he said. "What about lunch and a bike ride on a school day?"

"Sure," I said. "I guess I could do that. Except for the fact that I don't have a bike."

"Now," he said, "there's a problem I can fix."

17

SOMETHING WAS DIFFERENT. THE RUSTY METAL RAILINGS leading to my house were down. Not only down, but completely gone. I walked across the little lawn to the front walkway. Sure enough, the posts had been cut off almost down to the cement, then taped over with silver duct tape. The duct tape would probably keep my house from getting a spread in *Good Housekeeping*, but I was pretty sure it was a step up from the rusty metal railings.

The front lawn was completely free of rusted metal scraps, too. I could even see faint lines from the tines of a rake on the patches of dirt not covered by grass or dandelions.

I just stood there. It had been so long since anyone had done anything like this for me, I actually found myself wondering if some random metal railing thief was making his way through my neighborhood.

Cynthia's door slammed. "Hey, girlfriend," she yelled as she cut across her yard to mine.

"Aww," I said. "Did you do this?"

She giggled. "Actually, I only watched him."

The Huli Huli leftovers and everything else in the bag I was still holding were getting heavy. "Who?" I said.

Cynthia gestured toward my house with a swing of her bangs. "He left a note on the door. It's probably a love letter. Nice ass, by the way."

"*What* are you talking about?" I said.

"I'm certainly not going to let the cute guy out of the bag."
She headed back in the direction of her house. "You can't miss
it," she yelled over her shoulder. "It's tucked under the front
door."

I picked up the note on my way into the house and threw it
on the kitchen counter. I turned the burner on under the teakettle. I went to the bathroom. I made a mug of tea. Finally I sat
down at the kitchen table with my tea and opened the note. It
was written on a thin white rectangular napkin, the kind you
get with a take-out order. I turned it back over again on the table, the writing side down.

I closed my eyes.

Seeing Seth's handwriting again—the large, open letters
slanting optimistically to the right—made me remember the
note he'd left when he took off. It was a scrawl really, the last
note, so unlike the sweet love notes he'd sometimes leave under
my pillow on a birthday or anniversary, or next to the coffee-
maker on the kitchen counter of our tiny apartment when he
left for work while Anastasia and I were still sleeping.

That last note didn't say much, but the small, cramped letters, so rushed they barely grazed the paper, didn't even seem
as if they'd been formed by Seth's hand. During the first few
months after he was gone, I daydreamed an elaborate series of
fantasies all centering around the fact that maybe Seth hadn't
written the note voluntarily, or perhaps even written it at all.

Seth had been kidnapped at gunpoint by some crazy person, and the only way he could protect Anastasia and me was
to throw us off the trail with a hastily written note. He was on a
secret mission for something really important, and his specific
knowledge was key to the project. It was such a crucial project
that he hadn't even had time to write the note himself, but when
he got back, he'd explain everything, and it would all make
sense.

Other fantasies were less heroic. He'd been living a double life and had another family stashed somewhere. He couldn't take the duplicity anymore and the other family had won out. It was hard for me to picture his other kids being smarter or cuter than Anastasia, but I could easily imagine his other wife being less stressed and more fun. Maybe she was prettier, or maybe the sex was better, or at least more frequent.

After a while, I just stopped trying to figure it out. Seth was gone, and obviously, I'd never really known him at all. Without Anastasia as physical evidence that he'd at least pretended to love me and even married me, I might have even convinced myself I'd made him up.

One full week, exactly seven days, after Seth left, I lit a candle and held the note over it. I watched the flame eat its way through the paper, section by section, as I repositioned it. When my fingers started to burn, I went into the bathroom to get some tweezers so I could make sure every scrap turned to ash.

But by then, the entire note was seared forever into my brain:

I can't do this anymore. Tell Asia I love her. Sorry, Seth.

I picked up the new note. Everything in me wanted to burn it before I even read it. Maybe I could take it outside and borrow a little pink blowtorch from Cynthia so I could set it ablaze with a ceremonial flare. Maybe Seth would come back just as I was getting going, and I could turn the blowtorch on him, too. Not enough to disfigure him, since after all, he was Anastasia's father, but maybe to singe him a little. And to scare the shit out of him.

I wished I were a better person, but it was hard not to want to see him suffer.

There is a Hopi word *Oookywah* that roughly translated means, "I feel what you are feeling." The Hopis believe you can heal your suffering with the compassion in your heart.

I didn't have a clue what Seth was feeling now, or what he'd ever felt. I no longer even cared. To prove it, I turned the note over again and made myself read it.

Jill—
I had some extra time, so I got this started for you.
I taped over the rough edges so A. wouldn't get hurt.
I'll stop by to put the new railings up later this week
as time allows—will check first if I think you're going
to be home.

Wondering if I can come by this Sunday with some
Thai food? I won't stay long. Pls let me know.

Love to A.
Seth

It was time for the school bus. I walked out and sat on my front steps, trying to look past the carefully taped-off post holes and the neatly raked yard. They had nothing to do with me. Any gesture Seth made, today or forever, would be all about Anastasia.

The bus pulled down the street. The neighborhood kids exited in one big pack, then separated to go to their individual homes.

"Bye, Treasure," one of the kids yelled. "Bye, Asia."

That certainly hadn't taken very long.

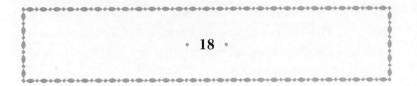

18

CLEARLY, I WAS OVERTHINKING. I'D TRIED TO TALK BILLY
Sanders into meeting me at Starbucks, but he'd insisted on
picking me up at my house. So I'd been going back and forth
about whether to invite him in when he got here, which could
be awkward, or whether I should be waiting in the front yard
when he pulled into my driveway, which might make me appear
overanxious.

I was wearing sneakers and my favorite jeans, plus the
third T-shirt I'd tried on. It was roomy enough that it wouldn't
ride up while I was on the bike, but not so loose as to be shape-
less. It was a shade of blue that was saturated enough that it
didn't make me look totally washed out, but not so dark that
it would get too hot. I'd been checking the weather reports
obsessively, and sun was the unanimous prediction.

It wasn't really a date.

It was simply lunch and a bicycle ride, or a bicycle ride and
lunch. Why hadn't I thought to ask Billy which one was first? I
knew he was picking me up at eleven, but what if we were going
to ride for two hours before we ate, and I didn't have enough
energy to keep up, not that I could actually imagine myself riding a bike for two hours, no matter what I had or hadn't eaten.
But still, maybe I should have at least a snack first. Though if
we went straight to lunch, then I'd have ruined my appetite.

I opened the refrigerator. There wasn't much in there, and
none of it looked the least bit appealing. I finally settled on an

apple and a piece of string cheese. I ate the apple while I paced around my little house, then put the string cheese back in the refrigerator. I went into the bathroom to brush my teeth again. I decided the blue T-shirt was the wrong shade after all, so I rummaged through my drawers until I found one in sky blue.

I pulled off the blue and put on the lighter blue. I bent over and touched my toes to test it out. I could feel it ride halfway up my back. I yanked it off and threw it on my unmade bed. I put the darker blue shirt back on again. I went into the bathroom and tried to undo the hair havoc wreaked by too many T-shirt changes.

I leaned forward and fluffed up my hair with my fingers. I stood up straight and flipped my head back. All I'd managed was to give myself some serious big hair. I looked like I hadn't left the house since the '80s. I patted my hair down closer to my scalp and this century.

I sat on the toilet and tried to pee, even though I didn't really need to. I washed my hands, avoiding my eyes in the mirror, so I didn't have to look at myself anymore. I didn't think I looked bad, exactly, but after all these years spent ignoring myself and focusing on my daughter, how could I possibly look good?

Maybe Billy Sanders simply wanted to sell me a bike.

At 10:50, I still hadn't decided whether to wait inside or outside. I ran into the bathroom and tried to pee one more time. I took my house key off the key ring. I also grabbed a twenty-dollar bill, so I could offer to pay my share at lunch, and my license and health insurance card, in case I got hit by a car while riding the bike. I put everything into separate pockets of my jeans, to balance the added bulk. I kept the key in one hand and my cell in the other, ready for a quick getaway.

I'd have liked to carry a few more things with me, maybe some tissues and lip gloss, even breath mints, but I was pretty sure fanny packs went out with big hair, and I didn't know what else I had that might work. Anastasia's old diaper bag? Her pink backpack from third grade? I knew it would look dorky to casually hook my purse over the handle bars. I also didn't think I could count on the bike having a wicker basket on the front, like the one that carried Toto in *The Wizard of Oz*.

A car beeped in my driveway.

"*Yoo-woo*," Cynthia yelled from outside my kitchen door a moment later.

I opened the door. For some reason I thought she was going to tell me Billy had changed his mind and couldn't make it.

"Hey," she said. "Wait till you see what the neighbor dragged in."

I followed her outside to her big gold SUV. She swung the huge rear door open with a flourish. "For you," she said.

"A kitchen sink?" I said, stating the obvious.

"Not just a *kitchen* sink. A *farmer's* kitchen sink." She smiled at me while she fixed her bangs.

She linked her arm through mine. "Hi-ho the derry-o," she sang as she spun me around. "A farmer for your kitchen."

It was a beautiful farmer's sink, a deep white porcelain rectangle with fluted lines in the front. Even used, it was probably worth a fortune.

"I can't take this," I said.

"You have to," Cynthia said. "It's a perfectly good sink, and I already made my client get rid of it."

I wondered how much it would cost to get a plumber to install it.

Cynthia leaned into the back end of the car. Her flowered tennis skirt rode up enough to show matching little flowered shorts underneath. I wondered if I could talk her into keeping the sink and letting me borrow a cute outfit to wear for my bike ride with Billy instead.

She grabbed one end of the sink. "Come on, hurry up. I haven't got all day."

It weighed a ton, but we managed to maneuver it to the center of my kitchen floor, where it sat like a beached white whale.

I stood up straight and smoothed out my T-shirt. Maybe the light blue would be better after all, as long as I was careful not to lean too far forward on the bike.

"So," I said. "Well, thanks for the sink."

Cynthia reached for her bangs. "Not a problem, girlfriend."

Just as Cynthia was going out the kitchen door, a red truck pulled into my driveway.

Cynthia let go of her bangs long enough to give a little wave. She turned to me. "Cute," she said. "Another husband?"

19

"I CAN'T BELIEVE YOU BROUGHT AN AKIRA FOR ME TO ride," I said. I turned sideways in the red pickup to get a better look at the red metallic bikes behind us. Their eerie eyelike handlebars peered back at me. "I just hope I don't get any scratches on it or anything. I have to warn you, I haven't been on a bike in practically forever."

Billy put on the blinker, then took a right. "You know what they say about riding a bike." He glanced over at me. "You'll be fine," he said. "And don't worry, it's a rental, so you and your Akira are both fully insured for damages."

"Great." I took another quick look behind me. The bed of the truck had a bike rack running the width of it. It looked like it could hold a whole row of bikes.

"So," I said. "Is this the truck you use for moving bikes to and from the rental kiosks?"

"One of them. We used to use trailer hitch racks, but the bikes are more protected in the bed of a truck, and I think it's actually easier to just lift the bike up and roll it into the rack, so we're definitely moving in this direction."

We were zigzagging down tree-lined back roads. I thought we were heading away from the ocean, but other than that, I had no idea where we were going. It was kind of nice not to have to be in charge for a change.

I rolled down the window and took a deep breath of spring

air. It was a perfect May day—crisp air, blue skies, flowers bursting into bloom.

"It's great to see you so relaxed," Billy said.

I turned and smiled at him. Once I got past agonizing over T-shirt choices, and forgot about the sink camped out on the floor in the middle of my kitchen, I did feel surprisingly relaxed.

Billy was wearing jeans and sneakers and a forest green short-sleeve knit shirt with an actual collar. What kind of guy wore bike shorts to business meetings but not bike rides?

Billy looked over at me. "What are you grinning about?"

"I was just wondering why you're so dressed up today."

"Thanks for noticing," he said. "I don't get this dressed up for just anyone."

A little laugh slipped out before I had time to think about whether he was kidding or not.

"You think I'm kidding, huh?"

"Sorry," I said.

He drove past a ball field, put on the blinker, and took a right onto a dead-end street. "I'm the one who should be sorry, I guess, but I'm warning you, this is as good as it gets. I gave all my ties to my wife's new husband."

"Did you really?"

"Well, metaphorically I did. In reality, he's got enough of his own to last a lifetime. And if he runs out, he's got my ex to buy him a new one every Valentine's Day."

"Where are we anyway?" I asked. Billy had pulled the truck into a wooded parking lot.

He put the truck into park and turned off the engine. "You always do that, by the way."

I put one hand on the door handle. "What?"

He took the key out of the ignition. It was attached to a big key ring filled with keys of all shapes and sizes. He spun it around his finger, then clipped it onto his belt loop. This might have made some guys look like a custodian, but on Billy, the outdoorsy carabiner-clip thing worked.

His raccoon eyes looked at mine again. "Well, you're the cultural expert, but it just seems to me that whenever someone tells you a little something about his life, the custom is that the other person responds in kind."

"Sorry," I said. "It's been a while." I pulled the lever to open my door.

"Whoa. Come on, one thing."

I clicked the door shut. "Okay, my ex-husband hated ties, too."

Billy reached for his sunglasses. "Perfect," he said. "I feel like I know you better already."

"Wise guy," I said. I opened the truck and jumped out.

Billy opened the back of the truck and climbed up. He lifted the bikes down to me, then handed me the helmets. Finally, he lowered a backpack and swung himself over the side of the truck like a cowboy at a rodeo, not that I'd ever been to one. I walked around and closed the gate at the back of the truck.

I managed to kick up the kickstand and stand astride my Akira without embarrassing myself.

"Wait," Billy said. "Here, sit on the seat. I just want to make sure it doesn't need to be adjusted."

I stood on my tiptoes and straddled the seat.

"Okay, now put one foot on the pedal." He put one hand lightly on my right knee.

I felt such a spark that I was surprised my right leg didn't kick out the way it does when the doctor checks your reflexes at a physical. I tried my best to stay calm and not tip the bike over.

"Now straighten out your leg as far as it can go," he said. His hair had a clean, unfussy smell, and up close you could really see the streaks of gray mixed in with the medium-brown strands. "Perfect. When your leg is fully extended, you should have just a slight bend in your knee."

I felt ridiculously disappointed when he finally let go. He handed me a helmet and strapped on his own. Then he reached down and laced his arms through the backpack. Finally, he pushed up the kickstand on his own bike.

"I'm a Libra," I said. "I'm right-handed. My favorite color is blue. I'm an only child, and both my parents are dead. Now can I ask where we are?"

Billy grinned. "See, I knew you could do it. It's the back entrance to the state park. Almost nobody knows it's here. We thought about trying to put in a bicycle kiosk, but we didn't want to ruin the secret. It's got twenty-three miles of trails, all without passing a single car, so it's a great place to ride. And sorry about your parents."

"Thanks. We don't have to ride all twenty-three miles, do we?" My legs were tired just thinking about it.

"Relax. We'll just do a nice, easy little loop."

"Perhaps you'd care to define that before I fully commit?"

"Too late." Billy swung his leg over his bike expertly. I watched him glide across the parking lot to the start of the trail.

I unstraddled my bike and walked it across the parking lot after him. If Billy noticed I wasn't actually riding yet, he was gracious enough not to point it out.

He gestured toward the trail with one hand. "Ladies first."

I had a bit of a wobbly start, but once I got going I was fine. The trail was nice and wide, smoothly paved and relatively flat.

Billy rode up beside me. "Isn't this great?" he yelled.

I nodded, and he pulled ahead.

It was gorgeous. Leafy trees and vines were flowering on both sides, and beneath them, I could pick out ferns among vast quantities of unidentifiable green things. Once I thought

I saw a lady's slipper, something I'd only seen in photographs, blooming right at the edge of the trail.

The air smelled. fresh and green, and it was laced with the sharper, resinous smell of pine. Occasional huge boulders broke up the foliage like pieces of sculpture. I could hear birds calling out to one another even through my helmet, and when we passed a little stream, I caught sight of a couple of deer standing there drinking. They looked at me like I was no big deal.

It didn't take long to start noticing the muscles in my thighs, but it was a good feeling, like discovering body parts I'd forgotten all about. Billy kept to an easy pace, occasionally looking back at me to make sure I was still behind him. As soon as I got my balance, I was even comfortable taking one hand off the handlebar long enough to give him a quick thumbs-up.

Once you factor out sharing the road with cars—smelling their fumes, hearing their noise, and knowing any minute might be your last if one of them miscalculates and takes you out—bike riding is amazingly peaceful. I felt like I could ride forever, just following Billy, not thinking at all, taking a right or a left when he did. Just being.

I wasn't even that tired when Billy made a right turn signal and pulled over. But as soon as I saw it, I knew why we'd stopped. At the side of the trail, there was a drop-off to a pond flanked by three little benches.

"Aww," I said as I fumbled with my kickstand.

Billy was already taking off his helmet. "Time for lunch," he said.

I looked around. "They serve food here?"

He laughed. "They do if you're with me."

We made our way down and sat on the middle bench. Billy took off his sunglasses and looped them onto the front of his shirt. He unzipped the backpack.

I burst out laughing.

"Be careful," he said. "We sell these at our flagship store."

Velcroed to the inside of the front flap of the dark green backpack was a small round wooden cutting board. Behind that were two plastic plates. Directly across from those were neat little compartments holding knives, forks, spoons and a corkscrew in place. At either end of those, a green-and-white-striped cloth dinner napkin sat jauntily in an acrylic wineglass.

Billy raised an eyebrow. "It's our picnic backpack for two. It's called The Datenic."

"Catchy," I said.

"Thank you," he said.

He unzipped another compartment and pulled out a small baguette and a triangle of Brie, and placed them between us on the bench. Next, he removed two bottles of water.

He handed me one. "I guess wine would have been more impressive, but I never drink and ride."

"This is impressive enough," I said. "And the bike I'm riding is probably much safer this way."

He raised his eyebrow again. "I factored that in."

We grinned at each other until I finally looked away. "It's so beautiful here," I said.

When I looked at him again, he was holding up his water bottle in my direction. "To new beginnings," he said.

I couldn't think of anything to say, so I just tapped my water bottle to his.

He turned and reached for the backpack. The ripping sound of Velcro completely cracked me up.

"Sorry," I said. I reached for one of the cloth napkins and dabbed at my eyes.

He held the little wooden cutting board as if he were going to throw it at me. "You're not going to make this easy, are you?"

"Sorry," I said again. "I really am sorry. It's a beautiful backpack. What's it called again?"

Billy shook his head. "Cute," he said.

I picked up the triangle of cheese and started peeling back the foil. He started breaking off hunks of bread.

We chewed for a while in silence. A couple of ducks floated by on the pond in front of us, and beyond them I could see a lily pad with a single pink flower in bloom.

"I can't believe how much I'm eating," I said. "This is the best bread and cheese I've ever had in my entire life."

Billy finished chewing and reached for his water. "Bike riding will do that for you. So, why is it that your ex isn't in the picture as far as your daughter goes?"

A cloud stopped in front of the sun. "Does that look like rain?" I asked.

Billy shook his head.

I took a deep breath. "Actually, he's back in the picture. At least he says he wants to be. He just saw her on Sunday for the first time in seven years."

"Whoa, that's a big deal."

He broke off another hunk of bread and handed it to me, then another for himself.

I nibbled at it and waited for the sun to come out again.

"How did it go?" Billy asked.

Maybe this bike ride wasn't such a good idea after all. Lives were so complicated, how could you ever explain yours to another person? Where would you start? What parts would you leave in and out? And even if you managed to find the energy to dredge it all up and lay it out between you, what was the guarantee that the person you were telling wouldn't turn out to be worse than the person you were talking about?

I sighed. "You mean besides the awkward part?"

"Seven years, it's gonna be awkward. How did he and your daughter do together?"

"Like two peas in a pod," I said. "They've been on the phone every night since then."

"That's good, right? I mean, is there any reason he shouldn't be around her?"

My eyes filled up and I blinked back the tears. "What if he abandons her again?"

Billy draped an arm across the back of the bench and gave my shoulder a squeeze. "I'll take him out."

"Thanks," I said. "That's really macho of you."

"I'm a macho kind of guy. Listen, the thing to hang on to is that there's going to be a lot of shit to go through, but once you get to the other side, the best is yet to come."

I turned to look at him. "How do you know that?" A tear escaped and trickled down my cheek.

Billy wiped it away. And then he kissed me.

20

ANASTASIA PLOPPED SOME OF THE CASSEROLE I'D MADE with community center leftovers onto her plate and handed me the serving spoon. The phone rang. I sighed and reached for my headphone. I'd probably jinxed myself by taking it off, hoping to get through dinner in peace.

"Great Girlfriend Getaways," I said. "Feisty—"

"Sorry to interrupt you, ma'am, but I was hoping I could interest you in a picnic backpack for two."

I giggled like a teenager.

Anastasia looked up.

"Does it have a name, sir?" I asked.

"It does, ma'am."

I motioned for Anastasia to start eating. "Is that something you can share with me?"

"Yes, it's called The Datenic."

"Very catchy. You know, I might actually have a need for something like that in my life."

Anastasia was watching me, her empty fork hovering in the air. I pushed myself away from the kitchen table.

"Why, thank you, ma'am. I was hoping you might feel that way."

I stepped over Cynthia's sink on my way to the living room. "Hey," I whispered. "I'm so glad you called, but we're eating dinner, and I'm also right in the middle of my phone shift."

"Okay, I'll let you go then. Dinner and a movie this weekend? Ex-husband babysits?"

I closed my eyes. "I'm just not ready to leave her alone with him yet."

"No pressure. What about another bike ride next week?"

I looked over my shoulder to make sure Anastasia hadn't followed me. "Sure," I whispered. "Can we start where we left off?" I actually sounded flirty. I was so proud of myself.

"You bet," he said. "And if you forget where that was, I'll remind you."

My feet barely touched the ground on my way back to the kitchen. "Hey, sweetie," I said. I sat down at the table and reached for the casserole.

"Was that my dad?" Anastasia said.

I laughed. It sounded forced, almost like a croak. "No. No. It was just a friend."

Anastasia's hazel eyes looked exactly like Seth's. "What friend? And what do you need in your life?"

I'd had this half-baked fantasy that I was going to tell her about Billy tonight. One little mention, maybe something about the cool bikes his company made or the fact that I was helping him get ready for a trip to Japan. Just enough to establish his existence, and then I could slowly and gradually build from there.

"An old friend I haven't talked to in forever," I said. "We were just joking around. I can't even remember what she said."

My cell phone rang. "Great Girlfriend Getaways," I said into the headphone. "Feisty and fabulous man-free escapes both close to home and all over the world. When was the last time you got together with *your* girlfriends?"

"Hello," a woman's voice said. "We've got your spring and summer catalog, but my friends and I can't decide which trip to take. None of us ever gets to go anywhere, and it's not like we have money to burn, so this is a big deal for us."

I nodded. "I hear you," I said encouragingly. Anastasia adjusted her pink headband without taking her eyes off me.

"So, I mean, if you could only take one trip, and you have no idea if you'll ever be able to do something like this again, which one would you pick? The Goddess Golightly Tour of Sedona? Mining the Mystical in Celtic Culture? I forget, is that one Ireland or Boston?"

"Ireland," I said. "But we've also got our Finessing the Freedom Trail with your Female Friends trip to Boston if you're looking for something closer to home."

Anastasia shook her head. She picked up her plate and stood up.

I stamped my foot.

She ignored me. She stepped over the kitchen sink on her way to the living room.

"And don't forget Shop Till You Drop in Europe," I said, "where you and your girlfriends will get to stay in hotels adjacent to all the best shopping districts of France and Italy. And there's also a side trip to the outlet stores in Mendrisio, Switzerland."

The woman sighed. "It's just so hard to decide. I mean, what if you choose one, and then you find out that another might have been even better?"

I covered the mouthpiece while I swallowed. "Here's the thing," I said. "Any one of them could be the trip of a lifetime."

The woman let out a puff of air. "That's helpful."

I closed my eyes and visualized biking with Billy, maybe through the Chianti countryside south of Florence, stopping along the way to tour a winery or have lunch in a small *ristorante*. Then I pictured us biking through the winding back roads of Ireland's rural west coast, watching sheep grazing near stone cottages, taking a break to hang out at a local pub. I mean, as long as I was with Billy, it was six of one and half a dozen of the other as to which trip would be better.

I opened my eyes. "What I'm trying to say is, when it comes right down to it, it's not where you go, or what you do, that matters so much as who you do it with. So, as long as you've picked the right friends, any of our trips could work for you."

"Easy for you to say," the woman said. "You probably get to go on all of them for free. Never mind, we'll figure it out ourselves."

"SPELLING TIME," I said to Anastasia as soon as we'd cleared the table and loaded the dishwasher, and she'd finished her other homework. "Do you want to do it with me or on the phone with your dad?"

Anastasia looked at me like I had three heads. "Dad," she said. "Don't you have to use the phone for work though?"

"If I miss anybody, I can always call back. Just don't take too long." I unplugged my headphone and handed my cell to her. "Oh, and tell your dad it's okay for him to come over on Sunday. And that Thai food is fine."

A minute later Anastasia was sitting at the kitchen table with her pink and purple pen and a sheet of paper in front of her, laughing on the phone with Seth. "Mom," she yelled. "Dad wants to know what kind of Thai food you want."

"Whatever," I said from the living room. It was right next to the kitchen, and the house was so small it's not like I needed to yell to be heard.

I was stretched out on the couch with my feet up on the old trunk. I was imagining biking through the western countryside in Japan with Billy, after we'd closed the deal for new Akira bicycle kiosks in Tokyo. We were triumphant. We were a team. We were taking a little victory tour before we headed home together.

"She likes shrimp pad thai, but vegetarian is fine if it's too expensive," I heard Anastasia say from the other room. "And she likes to get flowers, too. Especially daisies. You can pick them from the field next to my school. I can show you if you want."

I sat up straight and put my feet on the floor. Surely Anastasia couldn't possibly think that flower exchanges of any kind were in Seth's and my future.

Anastasia and Seth moved on to her spelling words, and I stretched out on the couch again. Maybe instead of biking around western Japan, Billy and I would stay in Tokyo. I'd try to get us a deal on a romantic corner room with a view of Mount Fuji.

"*Believe*," Anastasia said from the kitchen. "I believe you can live happily ever after. *Believe*."

I couldn't hear Seth's sentence, but whatever it was made Anastasia giggle.

"*Again*," Anastasia said. "Mom and I are glad you're coming over for dinner on Sunday again. *Again*."

Okay, so maybe she had a little bit of a fantasy going that Seth and I might get back together. Any kid in her situation probably would. It would just take some time for everything to sort itself out.

"*Brought*," Anastasia said. "If you brought me a kitten and my own phone, I would be the happiest girl in the whole wide world. *Brought*."

I breathed a sigh of relief. Anastasia was a typical ten-year-old girl. She was fine.

Just to be sure, I waited until I knew she was sound asleep. Then, addict that I was, I snuck into her room to find her diary.

Dad brings a boukay of daisies for my mom

And then he moves back

Into our house

So we have to buy a bigger

Yellow house with sunny windowsils for my new pet kitten

21

"HEY, KIDDO," JONI SAID. SHE WAS SITTING AT HER DESK with a pile of paperwork in front of her. I leaned over and gave her a hug, then rolled a chair up beside her.

"So, what do you need?" I asked.

Joni ran both hands through her crisp gray hair. "A pomegranate martini?"

"Now there's a thought," I said.

Joni shoved the papers aside and pulled up a file on the computer. "Can you send out an e-blast to our list about Shop Till You Drop in Europe and also make it our Web feature? I'd really like to fill that one."

"Done," I said. I reached for a piece of computer paper and started making notes. "Then you want me to take Costa Rica off the home page?"

"Yes, bury it. And I think we're going to have to break down and place an ad for another group leader. We're way over our promised ratio."

I made another note. "Got it."

Joni stoood up and grabbed two bottles of water from the tiny office refrigerator.

"Thanks," I said. I opened mine and took a big sip. "So, any news on the selling front?"

"Ha," Joni said. She put her Skechers-clad feet up on the desk and leaned back in her chair like she was twenty. "Women are still traveling, so we're making money, but in this economy, everybody's going to assume that if I'm selling, something must be wrong with the company. It's going to take the right buyer."

I didn't know I was going to say it until it came out of my mouth. "What about Sanders Family Bicycles? You know, the company that has all the bike kiosks?"

Joni swung her feet off the desk. "Now there's an interesting thought. What made you think of them?"

I could feel a blush sneaking up on me, so I flipped my hair out from behind my ears. "I've been, um, doing some consulting work for one of the owners. He's exploring the possibility of bicycle kiosks in Japan, and it just seems like they're a company that's, I don't know, open."

Joni grinned. "Looks to me like Japan is not the only possibility that's being explored."

I laughed noncommittally. A part of me wanted to tell Joni about Billy, but a bigger part of me was afraid it wouldn't hold up to the light of conversation. I wanted to envelop the whole idea of us in bubble wrap to keep it safe while it had a chance to grow.

"Moving on," I said. I took another sip of water.

Joni was still smiling. "It's a great company, but what would they want with GGG?"

"Well," I said. "I hear they're trying to balance some cuts they've made by investing in future growth. So, why not expand with a travel piece? They could keep GGG essentially the same, with the addition of bike tours, and also use its resources to add a new tour niche for families. Maybe pitch a special that if you take a bike trip with your entire family, you'll get a coupon for a discounted women-only trip to recover from the experience."

"Hmm," Joni said. "It's worth a shot—I'll reach out to them."

I felt a flash of disappointment. I mean, after all, it was my idea, so shouldn't I do the reaching out? But, then again, maybe Billy and I should keep business out of things for the time being. We had a long road ahead of us, and we could take our time weaving our lives together into a glorious mixture of travel and fun.

Soon enough, business and pleasure lines would blur. Our blended families would get along beautifully, too, and when people asked how we handled spending every holiday traveling together to exotic locations all over the world, I'd try not to look smug.

"Well," I'd say. "We both simply made the decision to divorce each other, but not our families. We're actually a lot like siphonophores. You know, animals made up of a colony of organisms that work together? We're separate, but we all still clump together."

I could almost picture it, although in my vision Billy's ex-wife didn't have a face, and Seth only showed up for dinner by himself on Sundays while Billy was conveniently out mowing the lawn or something.

Joni cleared her throat and brought me back to reality. "How's Anastasia doing with her dad?" she asked.

Anastasia's last diary entry appeared before my eyes in bright purple. I shook my head to dislodge it.

"Fine," I said. "Well, except for the fact that she's fantasizing about Seth and me getting back together."

"I'd say that's probably pretty normal."

I nodded. "That's what I was hoping."

Joni leaned forward in her chair. "But, then again . . ."

"What?" I said.

Joni's watery blue eyes looked right through me. "Well, there's always the chance that Anastasia's right, and you will get back together. Stranger things have happened."

I jumped to my feet. "Bite your tongue," I said.

Joni stood up, too. She put her hands on my shoulders. "Lovey, it's just that you've got to sort out the mess before you take the exit door. Otherwise you'll only drag it with you, and it'll clutter things up at your next stop along the road."

"Of course," I said. "I mean, I know that."

Joni gave me a kiss on my forehead.

I gave her a quick hug.

I screwed the cap back on my empty water bottle and threw it in the recycle bin. "Okay, that's it," I said. "I'm out of here. My big mean boss just gave me a ton of work to do."

ON MY WAY HOME, I made quick stops at the library and the grocery store. I pulled into my driveway minutes before Anastasia's bus was due to arrive.

My new railings were fully installed. "What?" I said out loud.

I put my car into park and climbed out. The white paint could use some touching up in a few places, but other than that, they looked amazing.

Not only did I have crisp white wooden railings leading up to my front door, but my whole house suddenly looked adorable. It actually looked like a house I would have bought even if I wasn't looking for the cheapest one I could find.

I couldn't stop looking at it. This was a house that would hold a perfect little family: perfect mother, perfect father, 2.5 perfect little children. They'd spend Saturdays raking the yard and power washing the siding, and when they were finished with the weekend chores, they'd go out for pizza and a movie on Saturday night.

Or they'd leave the well-adjusted, never-been-traumatized perfect little children with a babysitter who was on the honor roll at school, and fluent in at least two languages. Instead of plugging them into the TV so she could sneak her boyfriend into the house, the babysitter would play games with them all evening. Old-fashioned board games like Chutes and Ladders, Scrabble, Monopoly.

I unloaded everything from my car, happy for a chance to check out the railings again with each trip past. I knew Seth was responsible, but I was kind of half imagining that Billy had been the one to put them up. He would have noticed them propped up against my house when he picked me up for our bike ride, and then somehow managed to sneak over while I was out to put them up to surprise me.

Life with Billy would be like that: both of us solidly and predictably there for each other, but also always on the lookout for ways to surprise and delight.

I put the groceries away, then went back out to sit on my front steps and admire the railings some more.

"Hey, girlfriend," Cynthia yelled from about three feet away.

I jumped. "Geez," I said. "I didn't even see you."

"I know. I could have knocked you over with a fender."

"I bet," I said. I nodded in the direction of the railings. "So, how do you think they look?"

Cynthia gave me a thumbs-up with the hand not corralling her bangs.

The bus rolled down the street and stopped in front of my house. "Hey," Cynthia said. "You don't want to go away for a spa weekend, do you? I mean, I'm all for family bondage and everything, but the kids are wearing me out."

"Sure," I said. "Any time you have a client looking to get rid of a gift certificate, let me know."

The bus driver opened the door, and I waited for a glimpse of Anastasia. Cynthia's youngest, Parker, stepped off first. He ran over and threw his backpack at Cynthia, then took off in the direction of their house.

"Parker," she yelled. "Get back here right now!"

Parker kept running.

Cynthia bent down and picked up the backpack. "Don't be surprised if you find yourself looking for another backpack to throw, young man," she yelled.

She turned to me. "I almost picked you up some vertigo blinds my client was getting rid of this morning, but I think we should only go for high-end hand-me-downs."

"Vertical," I said. I mean, how could Cynthia build her business if no one corrected her when she misspoke?

"Vertigo," Cynthia said, "is what they give me. And, just for future reverence, if you absolutely have to wear that shirt with those pants, stay home."

22

LOY KRATHONG IS TRADITIONALLY CELEBRATED IN THAI-
land on the full moon night of the twelfth lunar month, which
usually falls in November. Even though it was May, Anastasia
and I decided to make it our dinner theme anyway, since it
would go with the Thai food Seth was bringing.

I loved the beauty and simplicity of Loy Krathong. *Loy*,
sometimes spelled *Loi*, means "to float," and *krathongs* are the
lotus-shaped receptacles that hold lighted candles and incense
as they drift on the water. During the festival, people all over
Thailand gather beside canals and rivers, light their candles,
and add coins to their *krathongs*. Then they silently make a
wish, place their *krathongs* in the water, and let them go.

It had been Anastasia's idea to fill the farm sink sitting in the
middle of our kitchen floor with water. She made a *krathong* by
gluing some packing peanuts to a piece of Styrofoam and then
painting her creation until it looked loosely like a purple lotus.
She placed some floating candles, shaped like little sunflowers,
around the *krathong*, and then pulled a dandelion flower apart
and sprinkled its narrow yellow petals over everything.

The water turned purple almost immediately. It was probably going to be a nightmare to clean up, but I had to admit it
looked sweet in a messy kind of way. I also thought it was an
added bonus that Cynthia's sink had finally come in handy for
something other than tripping over.

"Make a wish, Mom," Anastasia said. She handed me a penny from the penny dish in our kitchen junk drawer.

I closed my eyes. I wished for Anastasia to sail smoothly through the rest of her life. I wished for Seth to never disappoint her. I wished to somehow find a way to connect my life to Billy's. I wished for a plumber to install the kitchen sink.

It was probably more than a penny's worth of wishes.

"So, what did you wish for?" I asked when I opened my eyes.

"I can't tell you," Anastasia said. "Or it won't come true."

She moved into the living room to sit on the back of the couch and look out the window while she waited for Seth. I hadn't been able to talk her out of wearing her fanciest dress. It was pink and linenlike, sleeveless with a wide white collar and a white satin bow. We'd bought it when Anastasia played a princess in her class play last year.

It was getting snug around the armpits, and I'd barely managed to zip up the long zipper in the back, so I guess it didn't really matter if she got Thai food on it. And she really did look like a princess. I'd put her hair into a high ponytail and tied three long pink ribbons around the elastic. They fluttered when she moved her head, adding to the regal effect.

Seth wasn't due to arrive for another ten minutes, but it still broke my heart to see Anastasia watching and waiting for him. I couldn't help imagining the day he just wouldn't show.

She'd be sitting and sitting, checking the big old clock on the living room wall again and again. Then she'd start making excuses for him—maybe he'd lost track of time, maybe he was stuck in traffic, maybe he couldn't find his car keys.

Anastasia would begin to worry that Seth had been in an accident. And then, as the minutes ticked into hours, she'd get really worried. Finally, she'd insist I call the police and the hospital, and the whole time I'd be thinking: *I just knew he'd let her down. I knew it.*

"He's here!" Anastasia yelled. She jumped off the couch and practically flew out the front door.

I slid my feet into an old pair of flip-flops and followed at a more dignified pace.

By the time I got outside, Seth had already scooped Anastasia up into a big hug. He put her down on the ground, and she twirled around in her party dress. He put two fingers in his mouth and whistled a long *woo-hoo.*

Anastasia curtsied the way she'd curtsied in the play. "It's a little bit small because we bought it in third grade. I had to have it, because I got picked to be a princess."

"I can see why," Seth said. "You look exactly like a princess. Did you ever see *Star Wars*?"

"Only like a hundred times," Anastasia said. "But I'll watch it again if you want. I've seen the original trilogy and *The Clone Wars*. It's not as good, but at least it's animated."

Seth leaned into his car and pulled out a large take-out bag. He reached back in and handed Anastasia a shiny purple gift bag.

He finally noticed me. "Hey," he said. He was wearing jeans and another button-down shirt with the sleeves rolled up, this one with soft taupe pinstripes, so subtle they almost weren't there.

"Hey," I said. "Thanks for putting up the railings."

"The least I could do," he said.

"True," I said.

We looked at each other.

He grinned. "So, tell me what you really think, Jill."

Anastasia managed to wait until we got inside the house to open her present.

"Ohmigod," she screamed. "It's my very own Purple People Reacher Phone! My wish came true already!"

"You didn't," I said.

"Thank you, thank you, thank you," Anastasia yelled. She was jumping all over the kitchen floor. In another minute, she'd trip and fall over the kitchen sink, and we'd all end up in the emergency room for stitches.

"You're welcome," Seth said. He nodded at everything floating in the sink on the floor. "Did you do all that by yourself, Asia?"

"Yes!" Anastasia yelled. She was still jumping, and her ears had already turned red. "It's for Loy Krathong, and my wish came true *already*!"

I started putting plates on the table, so we could at least eat the Thai food before it got cold. Instead of offering to help, Seth sat down and started trying to clip the phone onto the sparkly purple lanyard that came with it.

"If you make a wish with someone on Loy Krathong," Seth said, "it means the person will be in your life forever."

Anastasia opened the penny drawer again. "Come on, Dad, let's make a wish."

I slammed a cabinet door shut. Seth and Anastasia both looked over.

"I meant you, too, Mom," Anastasia said. She held another penny out to me on her open palm.

"Thanks, honey," I said. I turned to Seth. "Don't you think you might have checked in with me first?"

"Why?" Anastasia said. "Why would we check in with you?"

I ignored her and waited for Seth to answer.

"I thought it would be a nice surprise," Seth said. "I know you need the phone for work, so it seemed like it would help out. I added Asia to my family plan—"

"Your family plan," I repeated.

"He's allowed to do that," Anastasia said.

"That way we'll have unlimited minutes together," Seth said. "And I got a great promotional deal on the phone. Plus, it's got a built-in GPS, which is an important safety feature for kids. I mean, we'll always know right where she is."

"Yeah," Anastasia said. "What's GPS again?"

I couldn't seem to stop myself. "Right," I said. "We haven't seen you in seven years, and now you want to know where she is."

I stomped off to the bathroom. I stared at myself in the mirror and tried to decide whether I wanted to spit or cry. A phone call to ask if the gift was appropriate would have been nice. A check to help out with the monthly bills would have been even nicer. It's easy to look like Santa Claus when you don't have to buy the groceries.

IT WAS THE SMELL OF THAI FOOD that brought me back to the kitchen. Anastasia and Seth had finished setting the table. They'd transferred the food from the take-out containers into bowls, something I had to admit Anastasia and I didn't always bother to do.

They'd also lit the little floating candles in the sink while I was gone and probably made a wish together, too. I made a silent little wish of my own that I could find a way to get through dinner without ruining it for all of us.

I sat at the table and took a sip of the wine Seth had already poured. It was a nice chardonnay, dry and oaky, the way I liked it.

Anastasia and Seth sat down, and Seth held up his glass. He smiled at me, and I did my best not to look away. "May you have warm words on a cold evening," he said, "a full moon on a dark night, and a smooth road all the way to your door."

Anastasia held up her milk. "And may you always have a Purple People Reacher Phone within easy reach!"

Seth touched his glass to hers. They both reached their glasses out to me.

I touched my glass to Anastasia's. "May your heart be light and happy," I said. "May your smile be big and wide. And may your pockets always have a coin or two inside."

Anastasia's face broke into a smile that was both big and wide. "Good job, Mom," she said.

"Thanks," I said. When I touched my wineglass to Seth's, it made a musical little clink.

Seth put his glass down and passed me the shrimp pad thai. "Your mother and I used to have toast contests," he said. "Mostly Irish, but any ethnicity would do in a pinch."

Anastasia reached for the chicken satay. "Tell me the story of how you met," she said.

I could feel Seth looking at me. I took a bite of pad thai, then a sip of wine.

"We met in Hiratsuka City, near Tokyo," Seth said. "We'd both gone there for Tanabata."

I concentrated on my pad thai.

Anastasia nibbled a bit of chicken off the skewer. "What's that?"

Seth put his glass on the table. "*Tanabata* means 'star festival.' It's a Japanese festival that takes place every year on July seventh. It's based on a Chinese folk legend about two stars, Vega and Alistair—"

"Altair," I said.

"Thanks," Seth said. "Anyway, *Altair* and Vega were lovers. All year long they were separated from each other by the

Milky Way, but once a year, on the seventh night of the seventh month, and only if it didn't rain, they could meet."

"Cool," Anastasia said. "What if it rained?"

"Then they'd have to wait for the next year," I said.

"There are Tanabata celebrations all over Japan," Seth said. "Sendai has one of the most famous ones, but that's way up in the north, so I went to Hiratsuka City, because it was closer, and so did your mom. The streets were all lit up and packed with people. And everywhere you looked, there were all these great big bamboo sculptures."

"People write their wishes on long strips of colored paper and hang them from the bamboo to make them come true," I said.

"That's how we found each other," Seth said. "I wanted to write a wish, but I didn't have a pen, so I turned around to borrow one from the prettiest girl there."

"What did the pen look like?" Anastasia asked.

"I don't remember," Seth and I both said at the exact same time.

We all laughed.

"I think it was from the tour company I was working for," I said. "I can't even remember the name of it anymore."

"If It's Tuesday, This Must Be Japan?" Seth said.

I shook my head. "Ohmigod, that was the worst job in the whole wide world. I never thought I'd survive it. If I hadn't met you that night . . ."

I closed my mouth, because I didn't have an end to the sentence. It was too vast, both the best and the worst of all things possible.

"What wish did you write, Dad?" Anastasia asked.

"I wished that the girl with the pen didn't already have a boyfriend."

I took another sip of wine and pretended I wasn't there.

Anastasia reached for another skewer of chicken satay. "Did your wish come true?"

"My wish came true," I heard Seth say, even though I was staring at the candles in the sink and trying not to listen. "It was the second most magical night of my life."

"What was the first?" Anastasia said.

I looked up at him.

Seth reached over and tickled Anastasia's cheek with her ponytail. "The night you were born, silly."

23

SETH YAWNED. HE STOOD UP, PUT BOTH HANDS ON HIS lower back, and stretched. "What time is it anyway?"

I yawned, too, then peeked in at the living room clock. The one on the stove had been broken since Anastasia and I'd moved in.

"Wow," I said. "It's almost midnight. I'm really sorry—I had no idea it was this late."

Seth rubbed his eyes. "That's okay. It's one of those jobs you pretty much have to finish once you start it. Thanks for letting me read Asia a bedtime story while you ran out to buy the sealer, by the way."

"I can't believe you got her to go to sleep," I said.

He smiled. "She conked right out while I was reading."

"I didn't realize you'd have to cut the counter to install the sink," I said.

Seth ran his hands across the fluted ceramic front of the sink. "It was worth it. This sink is a real beauty."

He put the pink saw back into Cynthia's silver and pink tool case. He snapped the lid closed and put it on the floor. "I have to admit, I was relieved to find out the Barbie tool case belonged to a neighbor."

We grinned at each other.

"Not my style," I said.

"I didn't think so."

Seth turned back to the sink. "Okay, let's test this baby out." He twisted the drain and turned on the cold water. We both stood there and watched the sink fill up.

Seth turned off the faucet. He picked up Anastasia's Styrofoam *krathong* from the kitchen counter and floated it on the water.

He reached his hand into the pocket of his jeans and pulled out some change. He handed me a penny.

When his hand touched mine, I pulled back as if I'd been stung, but I was already holding the penny.

I placed it in the center of the floating *krathong*. Seth put his penny next to mine. I wished for the courage to ask the question that had been burning a hole in my heart for the last seven years.

"Why, Seth?"

I waited for him to say *why, what?* Or even to turn and run.

He gave the *krathong* a little push across the sink. "You don't remember?"

Now I wanted to run, but I didn't. "Remember what?"

He turned and looked at me with tired hazel eyes. "God, Jill. You knew I wanted it to be the three of us. I kept asking and asking you to come with me. I was *suffocating*. I'd wake up in the middle of the night, and I literally couldn't breathe."

I was drawing a complete blank.

He rubbed his hand back and forth across the dark stubble on his jaw. "I mean, it wasn't the life we'd planned. We were going to keep traveling to exotic places until we found somewhere that felt just right and where we could make a difference. And suddenly, you're all about getting Asia wait-listed for preschool and never missing Sunday dinner at my parents'. And then, don't you remember, you wanted to move into their *basement*. . . ."

"Just long enough to save for a down payment on a house," I said. "And it's not like they didn't offer."

I crossed my arms over my chest. "I didn't think you were serious," I said. "I mean, I knew you *thought* you were serious. But I thought you just hadn't come around to facing reality yet. What if Anastasia got malaria? It was hard enough finding a good pediatrician here."

A cool breeze blew through the window over the sink, and the old white rolling shade made a snapping sound. I rubbed my bare arms to warm them up.

"I'd spent my whole life trying to break away from my family," Seth said.

"I'd spent my whole life trying to find a family," I said.

Seth made a sound that was almost a laugh.

I looked at him. "Why did you come back, Seth?"

He looked up. I followed his gaze. There was an ugly outdated light fixture in the middle of my kitchen ceiling. The carcasses of several trapped dead bugs were clearly visible behind the round frosted glass globe. I'd never noticed them before.

"Do you want the truth?"

I wasn't sure, but I nodded anyway.

Seth was still staring at the light fixture. "There was this woman. We'd been together for a while, a couple years, and then one day out of the clear blue sky she wanted to move back to the States, get married, and have kids."

"So, what," I said. "You thought you'd drop in again to invite Anastasia and me to the wedding? Or maybe you needed a flower girl?"

"Don't," Seth said.

I didn't say anything.

"It was this huge epiphany for me. I mean, how could I do that? I already had a family."

"Duh," I said.

I had no idea why I said it. Possibly too much time spent in the company of a ten-year-old. In any case, it cracked us both up. We laughed and laughed, in that slightly hysterical way that happens when your nerves have been strung tight for too long, and every time one of us would stop, the other would get us going again. A long time ago, Seth and I had laughed together a lot.

I pulled a sheet of paper towel off the roll and dabbed at my eyes. "So," I said casually. "Are you still with her?"

"No, we went our separate ways right after that. It's been over a year now."

Neither of us said anything. We stood there for a while. I was leaning back against the farmer's sink, and the fluted edges pressed into my back like ceramic ruffles.

"Well," I said finally. "Thanks again for putting in the sink."

Seth stretched. "Yeah, I should get out of here."

I turned to drain the water in the sink, and Seth went to walk past me at the same moment. We bumped into each other. I stepped right. Seth stepped left.

"Dance?" I said.

He put his hands on my shoulders.

When he kissed me, it was as if all the years just melted away. I knew the curve of his back; the ticklish spot behind his ear; the clean, earthy way he smelled. My brain shut down and let raw passion take over. He could have grabbed me by the hair and dragged me down the hallway to my bedroom like a caveman, and I would have loved it. Or, if he didn't, I would have clubbed him over the head and dragged him.

We made love in my messy bedroom quietly, careful not to wake our daughter. I flashed back to the times when she was a baby and we'd try to sneak off to the bedroom on the weekend, while she was taking a morning nap and we still had some energy before the day wore us down. We'd pull down the shades against the bright morning sun and make love quickly, furtively, a race against naptime.

Tonight, we ran our fingertips up and down each other's bodies as if we were reading seven years of Braille. Finally I curled up against Seth and fell asleep with his arms wrapped around me.

After a wedding in the Netherlands, couples sometimes plant lilies of the valley around their house so that they can celebrate the renewal of their love each time the blooms come around again.

I dreamed that Seth and Anastasia and I moved to Holland. We bought a tall, skinny brick house with steep winding stairs in The Hague. The house was in a row of attached brick houses that all looked the same from the front and had narrow walled brick gardens in the back.

Every day after school, Anastasia would join us in the garden, and the three of us would plant lilies of the valley together. Because we knew that even though the leaves and flowers of the plant were poisonous, somehow what we were really planting in Holland was happiness.

24

I WOKE UP JUST BEFORE MY ALARM WENT OFF. IF THE room hadn't smelled of stale sex, I might have been able to convince myself I'd dreamed the whole thing.

"Shit," I said out loud.

It was hard to tell whether I was talking about the fact that Seth was no longer in my bed or that he'd been there at all.

I jumped up and slipped into my ancient terry cloth robe. Maybe Seth wasn't really gone but only making pancakes or something. If so, I needed to get him out of here. Fast, before Anastasia woke up.

My kitchen was empty, other than the new farmer's sink. Its fancy fluted front seemed to undulate across the room at me like some porcelain cabaret dancer.

Clearly, I needed caffeine. I made my way over to the teakettle, careful not to look at any surface that might possibly be holding a note from Seth. Whatever had happened last night, whether it turned out to be the best thing that could have happened between us or the worst, I definitely didn't want to have to read about it in a note that would be seared into my brain for the *next* seven years.

I poured boiling water over an English Breakfast tea bag, because it was the strongest thing in my cupboard. I let it brew briefly, then gulped it down while it was still hot enough to burn my kiss-ravaged mouth.

As soon as the caffeine kicked in, I allowed my eyes to wander around the kitchen. I mean, just because there was a note didn't mean I had to read it. I could always simply cut to the chase and burn it right away.

The kitchen turned out to be note-free. I checked my bedroom—under the pillows, on top of the dresser, even the back of the door. Nothing. Nothing in the bathroom either.

I knocked on Anastasia's door. "Time to get up, Sweetie," I sang in a fake cheery voice.

And the whole time I was thinking: *This time I didn't even get a note.*

OF ALL DAYS, Cynthia had to pick today to be on time for the bus. She was already sitting on my front steps when I opened the door. Anastasia ran right past her to join the kids on the sidewalk.

"Hey," I said.

Cynthia crossed her spray-tanned legs at the ankles and pulled her tennis skirt down until it was only a mile or two from her knees.

I crumpled my way down and landed on the top step beside her in my ratty T-shirt and sweats.

"Woo," she said. "Late light over here last night. Looks like you partied till the cows came."

"Yeah, well, at least I got the kitchen sink installed."

Her eyes lit up. "Do you mind sharing the plumber?"

"Actually," I said, "he's all yours if you want him."

"Thanks, girlfriend," Cynthia said.

The bus pulled up. Anastasia checked her Purple People Reacher Phone flamboyantly as she climbed up the steps. She'd probably double, if not triple, her cool quotient by the end of the day, though she'd have to keep everything but the GPS and the emergency button on the phone turned off while she was at school. I remembered this from glancing at Rules for Cell Phone Use at Fraser Elementary School in the back-to-school packet, right before I pitched it. At the time I remembered thinking: *What kind of crazy parent would let her fourth grader get a cell phone?* Ha.

Anastasia disappeared without a glance my way and took a seat at the far side of the bus. I had the feeling I could disappear just as casually, and she'd never even miss me. She'd been daddy's little girl from the moment she'd heard Seth was back. It was as if all the time I'd been there for her had simply evaporated the minute he showed up. *Hey,* I wanted to yell after the bus, *remember me? The one who's been taking care of you all these years?*

Cynthia was already halfway back to her house by the time I noticed she was gone, so I dragged myself inside and jumped in the shower. I turned the hot water up until it was almost scalding and shampooed twice. The old song about washing that man right outta my hair floated into my head, but I couldn't quite bring myself to sing it.

I was trying not to think, to stay numb, but waves of anxiety kept rising from my stomach to my heart, and a little voice inside of me wouldn't shut up. *Just when you were finally moving on,* it moaned. *What were you thinking?* it groaned.

The last thing I needed was another faux trip to Thailand to trigger a few more flashbacks from last night, but I had neither the time nor the energy to come up with a Plan B for Lunch Around the World. I added Anastasia's *krathong* to the shopping bag on the counter. I'd already filled it with Styrofoam, paint, and brushes, and other supplies, as I'd multitasked for Monday's class while Anastasia and I were getting ready for Sunday dinner with Seth. I grabbed a handful of pennies on my way out the door.

I stopped at the supermarket for the ingredients for chicken and eggplant curry, plus some jasmine rice and mango sorbet.

Since there was room in the budget, I also added a bunch of cellophane-wrapped flowers as an upgrade to last night's dandelions. Then I wandered up and down the aisles, not really sure what I was looking for. Some essential ingredient that would make my mind stop racing?

I was late getting to the community center.

"*There* she is," T-shirt Tom said as I walked in. Today's shirt said I'M NOT GETTING SMALLER, I'M BACKING AWAY FROM YOU. I thought there might be a message there about my life, but I couldn't quite put my finger on it.

Ethel and one of her friends took the shopping bags out of my hands and placed them on the counter.

"Okay," I said, once the class was clustered around me in the kitchen. "So, well, today we're going to Thailand. Um. Thai food is all about the blending of four basic flavors that all start with the letter *s*." I counted them off on my fingers. "Sweet, sour, salty . . ."

I wracked my brain for the fourth one.

"Soy?" T-shirt Tom said.

I shook my head.

"Sugar?" one of his sidekicks said.

"That's the same thing as sweet," Donna said. Or maybe it was Bev.

"Shrimp?" someone said. "Don't they use a lot of shrimp in Thai cooking?"

Everybody was looking at me. I was lost. Completely and ridiculously lost. I wondered what would happen if I just picked up Anastasia's *krathong* and the pennies and left. Wait, music. I'd forgotten all about finding some Thai music.

"Spicy!" Ethel yelled.

"Thank you," I said. I opened the community center cupboard, took out a glass, and filled it with water. I drank it.

"Looks like somebody had a spicy night last night," T-shirt Tom said.

"Leave her alone," Ethel said. "Did you get back together with your boyfriend, honey?"

I had this sudden crazy urge to sit them all down and give them the long answer. I'd start at that first meeting at the Tanabata festival and tell the whole story of Seth and me, fast-forwarding a little through the bedroom scene last night, and ending with my note-less morning. I mean, between them all, they probably had centuries of experience in things like this. They could probably give me some really useful advice. They might even be able to tell me what the hell had happened. There might even be a name for it, other than *stupidity*.

When I put the empty glass on the pitted stainless steel counter, it made a metallic *ping*. I forced myself back into teaching mode again. I ignored the question and smiled at the class.

"Many of the dishes of Thailand combine all four of these flavors," I said. I thought about trying to repeat them for reinforcement but decided not to risk another brain freeze. "And, ideally, the flavors are harmoniously blended both within each dish and across an entire meal, which might consist of soup, a curry dish, and a dip with vegetables."

"Aren't curries from India?" somebody asked.

"*Curry* means gravy," I said, "and the origin of the word is from southern India, but curries are also made in Africa, the Pacific Islands, and throughout Southeast Asia. Thais are particularly known for making foreign recipes their own, and that's certainly true with curries."

A couple of them yawned, so I cut to the chase.

"Today we're going to make chicken and eggplant curry with *nam prik gaeng ped*, or spicy red curry paste, which is the most common of the curry pastes. It's a mixture of"—I picked up a tube of red curry paste I'd bought and read the ingredients—"dried chili pepper, garlic, shallots, galangal, lemongrass, coriander, peppercorn, cilantro root, salt, shrimp paste, and Kaffir lime zest."

I reached into the grocery store bag and pulled out a bunch of basil, some cans of coconut milk, a bottle of fish sauce, a family-size package of boneless chicken, and two enormous eggplants. I handed them out, and the students started passing them down the line, as if the community center was on fire and we were the bucket brigade.

"Ideally," I said, "you should use *bai horapah*, or sweet Thai basil, but any basil will do in a pinch. And in Thailand, the chicken wouldn't be boneless, because they would use the bones to add more flavor. Also, it's best to use Thai eggplants, which are about the size of golf balls, but they're hard to find, so we're going to use regular eggplants and just cut them into bite-size cubes."

I was back on track. I'd tell the story of Loy Krathong while half the class was cooking and the other half made a Styrofoam *krathong*. We'd wish on some pennies, eat, and then I'd pack up and get the hell out of here.

I reached into the other bag, the one I'd brought from home. When I pulled my hand out, instead of a piece of Styrofoam or some paint, I was holding a little white piece of paper. I turned it over to look at it, thinking I really needed to be more careful about saving my receipts to get reimbursed.

It was a note from Seth—fully formed letters, open loops, slanting optimistically to the right.

J—
I want us to be a family. See you and Asia tonight.

Love, S

25

I CALLED SETH THE MINUTE I GOT OUT TO MY CAR.

"Hey," he said when he answered his cell. "I've been thinking about you all day."

"About last night," I said.

"I know," he said. "It was amazing. I hope I didn't wake you up when I left this morning. I had an early appointment, and I needed to drive all the way back to my parents' house to shave and shower and all that stuff."

It occurred to me that I had no idea what Seth did for a living. He was practically a stranger.

"Can I pick up something for dinner?" he asked.

I leaned my head forward and conked it lightly on the steering wheel. Even in the throes of passion, I would have remembered dinner plans if we'd made them. I wondered if Seth had already packed his bags and loaded them into the trunk of his car.

There had to be a way to back things up a little, like maybe to the point of discussing the possibility of going out for coffee together sometime.

"Jill? Are you still there?"

That was a question to be pondered. Considered, contemplated, even brooded over at great length. It's not that I necessarily wasn't still there, but I needed to be sure I was moving forward and not backward in my life. And I definitely didn't want to feed Anastasia's burgeoning fantasies about her parents getting back together. I wanted her completely out of the loop until I knew for sure what was going to happen.

And, of course, there was also the matter of what to do about tomorrow's bicycle ride with Billy, which I had to admit, with or without The Datenic, was essentially a date. And I also had to admit, shameful as it might be for a woman who'd just slept with another man, I kind of wanted to see him again. At least I thought I did. And if I did, what a despicably disloyal thing I'd done by sleeping with Seth.

"Listen," Seth said. "One of us must be out of range, so I'm going to hang up now and try again in a minute."

I hung up, too, and just sat there and closed my eyes. Half a minute later the phone rang again.

I opened my eyes and answered on the first ring. "Dinner won't work tonight. I'm tired, and I have a lot to do, and I also have to work a GGG shift later. So, I'll talk to you soon, okay?"

There was a pause. "Sure. Tell Asia to call me when she's ready for her spelling, okay?"

"Sure," I said. "Okay, well, bye."

I clicked my phone off. I drove home. I tried not to think.

Heading straight for Anastasia's diary as soon as I walked in the door was probably not the smartest thing to do, but I did it anyway.

A my name is Asia

Seth and me and Jill went up the hill

In a spill we

All fell down

"GREAT GIRLFRIEND GETAWAYS," I said into my headphone.

"*Washed,*" Anastasia said into her Purple People Reacher cell phone. "This morning I washed my hands in the beautiful new sink my dad put in for us. *Washed.*"

"Feisty and fabulous man-free escapes both close to home and all over the world," I said. "When was the last time you got together with *your* girlfriends?"

"*Hamster,*" Anastasia said. "If I can't get a cat right away, I would settle for a hamster. *Hamster.*"

"Can you tell me more about your tour of Egypt?" a woman's voice was saying in my ear.

"*Always,*" Anastasia said. "When my dad reads me a bedtime story, I always have a good night's sleep. *Always.*"

I couldn't take it anymore, so I pushed myself away from the kitchen table.

"Excuse me," I said. "But I didn't quite catch what you said."

"Egypt," the woman said. "I asked about your Egypt tour. Is that something you're qualified to discuss? If not, I'll wait while you put me through to someone who is."

I rolled my eyes while I walked into the living room. I entertained myself along the way by making the angular arm movements from the old Bangles song, which somehow I still remembered from the mid-'80s.

I flopped down on the couch. "You'll be happy to know my qualifications are impeccable. Take it from me, our Walk Like an Egyptian trip is not to be missed. You and your girlfriends will cruise the Nile with a certified Egyptologist—"

"What's a certified Egyptologist?"

Actually, I had no idea, but I took a stab at it. "It's a tour guide who has studied Egypt for a very long time."

"You mean like centuries?"

"Exactly," I said.

"That was a joke."

"I knew that," I said. "Funny. Anyway, you'll also visit the temples of Luxor, Horus, and Karnak, and you'll even take a camel ride."

I stretched back on the couch and closed my eyes.

"Do you have to have riding experience?"

I opened my eyes again. "You mean like camel-riding experience?"

The woman laughed. "No, I meant do you have to know how to ride a horse before you take on riding a camel?"

I thought about it. "I'm pretty sure they're mutually exclusive skills," I said. "Previous llama-riding experience might be a plus though."

"That's a good point," the woman said. "I'll look into that."

I tried to imagine what life would be like if the biggest problem I had was where to find a llama-riding class. Maybe I'd save up to buy a few llamas and start my own llama farm. Anastasia could pretend they were oversize hamsters.

The woman cleared her throat. I jumped. I'd totally forgotten about her.

"It probably sounds like I'm overthinking this," she said, "but it's just that I'm the planner in the group, and I find that the more prepared we are for each trip we take, the more my friends and I get out of it."

"I can see that," I said. "How often do you take trips?"

"At least once a year. More if we can swing it."

"Wow," I said. "So, I guess none of you has kids, huh?"

"Sure we do. It takes some juggling, but it's worth it. And if you don't spend time with your friends, where are you going to be when your kids grow up and leave you?"

"Can I come with you?" I heard myself say.

"Excuse me?"

"Kidding," I said. "I was just kidding."

As soon as I hung up, I peeked into the kitchen. Anastasia had her Purple People Reacher Phone tucked between her ear and her shoulder and was still writing away with her fluffy pen.

"*Missed*," she said. "I missed seeing you at my house when I got home from school today. *Missed*."

I turned around again. I wasn't going to think about it. I was going to go into the bathroom, wash my face and brush my teeth. With luck, Anastasia would be off the phone when I got back, and we'd both be asleep by nine o'clock. I'd be the one with the covers over my head.

It had taken Seth seven years to show up again, and even if it hadn't taken me much more than a couple of seconds to jump into bed with him, there was no rush to figure out anything else. Dinner on Sundays was plenty for now.

I pictured myself sitting at a sidewalk café one day, telling this story to a friend I traveled with, at least once a year, more if we could swing it. *So*, I'd say, *just when I'd finally met this cute guy who owned a bike company, my ex-husband, who had completely broken my heart when he abandoned me and my daughter seven years before, shows up. I mean, I'd had one date with the new guy and even kissed him, but then suddenly I found myself in bed with my ex.*

I'd sip my tea, flip my hair back, and laugh.

My friend would lean forward, all ears. *So*, she'd say, *what happened?*

And by then I'd know.

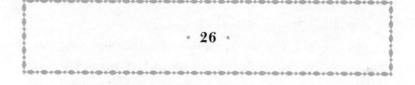

26

I MADE SURE I WAS WAITING ON THE FRONT STEPS WHEN Billy pulled into my driveway. I couldn't shake the feeling that if I let him into the house, he'd somehow know about Seth. Not that I owed him an explanation. Not that what I did on my own time was any of his business. Not that I was feeling guilty as hell. Not that I had a clue how to handle any of this.

I stood up, pulled down my T-shirt, yanked up my jeans discreetly, and walked toward the red pickup truck. I watched Billy put it into park. Even through the tinted window, I could see that he was smiling.

I gave him a little wave. He started to open his door.

"That's okay," I said. "I can get my door."

I kept walking. Billy climbed out anyway. He was wearing jeans and another short-sleeved knit shirt with a collar, this time blue. I thought shirts like this were best left to golfers, and on Billy they looked incongruous, even borderline geeky. I wondered if he'd bought one in every color, and called it a wardrobe. Or maybe his kids gave him another one every Father's Day, now that he and their mother were divorced and he no longer had to wear ties.

Billy reached around me and opened the passenger door. He even smelled outdoorsy. Either he'd just finished mowing the lawn, or spending so much time outside had seeped into his pores.

"Thanks," I said.

"It's good to see you," he said. He leaned in for a kiss.

I turned my head and kissed him on the cheek. "You, too."

Just as there is no graceful way to avoid a kiss on the lips, there is no graceful way to get into a pickup truck. I grabbed the doorframe with both hands and hoisted myself up. I felt Billy's hand on the small of my back. I focused on ignoring the little shower of sparks his touch set off while I found the seat belt. He shut my door and walked around to his own.

I turned sideways and checked out the two red metallic Akiras in the rear of the pickup. "What, no Datenic?" slipped out of my mouth before I could stop it.

Billy laughed. "After all the abuse you gave me last time? I'm sorry, but it's going to have to be a Datenic-free date this time."

"Aww," I said.

As soon as I said it, I regretted it. Instead of acknowledging that this was a date, what I should have done was to casually say something that would dial this back from a date to a pre-date. I mean, what was the rush? Why couldn't we just be bike buddies for a year or two?

Billy stretched his arm across the back of the seat and turned to back out of my driveway. The band on his sleeve gripped his biceps, and the muscles of his forearms looked strong and sinewy.

I turned away and stared out my window.

"I was thinking we could ride first, then go out to lunch. There's this great little off-the-beaten-path courtyard café I want to take you to, if that's okay."

"Sure," I said, because I couldn't quite think of a polite way to say, *You know, I think I'd prefer somewhere just a tiny bit less romantic than an off-the-beaten-path courtyard café today. If that's okay.*

I rolled down the window. It was another beautiful day. Not a cloud in the sky. Though, really, that could change anytime.

One minute you'd have a perfect day, and an hour later the sky could open up and it would be pouring.

We zigzagged along the same tree-lined back roads we'd taken last time. Billy turned on the radio and started switching stations. He stopped when he came to Van Morrison singing "Brown Eyed Girl." He started singing along. His voice wasn't that great.

Maybe the trick was to nudge things back to business. "So," I said. "What's the latest on Japan? Did you meet with your go-between yet?"

"Yeah, we've met, and things are really moving. The guy's great. He's got some meetings set up already, so it looks like we'll be heading to Tokyo next month."

"Wow," I said. "That was fast." I hoped I didn't sound as left out as I felt. I could actually feel disappointment sitting like a rock in my stomach.

We drove past the ball field, and Billy put on the blinker. We took a right onto the dead-end street that led to the back entrance to the state park.

Billy pulled into the wooded parking lot. He put the truck into park and turned off the engine. I pushed the release button on my seat belt and reached for my door handle.

"Wait," he said.

"What?" I said.

I turned.

He leaned across the long black leather seat. He put one hand firmly on each of my shoulders. "I just wanted to say I've been thinking about you all week," he said.

I leaned back. The door opened. I screamed.

He grabbed me by the wrists and yanked me back just before I fell out.

"Whoa," he said. "That was close."

"No kidding," I said.

He was still holding my wrists.

"Are you okay?" he said.

"Listen," I said. "I can't do this."

He let go of my wrists. He took off his sunglasses and placed them on the dashboard. He looked at me with his raccoon eyes. "What's up?"

I buried my face in my hands and shook my head back and forth. "I'm a mess. I don't know what I want. I'm not even sure I know who I am. And I think I might have, I mean, I. I. I."

I looked up.

Billy smiled. "Ay yi yi?"

"Yeah, pretty much." He had a great smile. He was such a nice guy. Why hadn't I remembered that before I jumped into bed with Seth?

"Come on, it can't be that bad."

"Ha," I said.

Billy reached over and took the keys out of the ignition. "Then how about we ride first and talk later. Things always look better once you get a few miles in."

He handed the bikes down to me, and then the helmets. He swung himself over the side of the truck with an easy athleticism that was hard not to admire.

I strapped on my helmet. When I straddled my metallic red Akira, its eerie eyelike handlebars peered up at me.

"What are *you* looking at?" I whispered.

Billy let me set the pace. I rode as hard as I could along the smooth, wide surface. The shady trail was cool and comforting, a welcome relief from the bright light of day.

The growth on either side of the path seemed greener and lusher than even a week before. I breathed in the rich smells of pine and what I thought might be honeysuckle in bloom. I pushed my pedals harder and welcomed the burning sensation in the center of my thighs.

I had this crazy thought that maybe I could keep riding, for a few months, even years, until my life sorted itself out. Anastasia could ride with me when she wasn't at school, or sleeping or eating or doing her homework, but the rest of the time I'd just keep pedaling solo.

Maybe I could set up a stationary bike to make it more practical. I'd just keep pedaling and pedaling all day, like a hamster on its wheel. If I put the bike in the middle of the kitchen, it would make it even more practical, since I could just reach over and cook dinner at the same time. And answering my GGG calls would be a piece of cake. Lunch Around the World might be a little more problematic, but I'd think of something.

My T-shirt was sticking to my back, and I could feel beads of sweat on my forehead. My lungs were starting to burn, and my right knee made a little clicking sound about every third rotation. The bicycle seat was getting harder by the minute, and the center of each cheek of my buttocks had a burning spot to match the ones in my lungs. The muscles in my forearms were feeling overworked and underappreciated.

Billy rode up beside me. "Up to you, but you might want to take it down a notch or two," he yelled. "Or you could regret it in the morning."

It wouldn't be the first thing I'd regretted in the morning.

I turned to him. I took a ragged, fiery breath.

"I slept with my husband," I yelled.

And then I crashed.

27

WE WERE SITTING AT THE OUTDOOR CAFÉ, AND I HAD MY leg propped up on an extra chair. A cloth napkin wrapped around a Baggie filled with ice was resting on my knee, which felt frozen and flaming at the same time, like it might turn into Baked Alaska just in time for dessert.

"I can't believe I didn't even see it," I said.

"Those branches come at you like that sometimes." He leaned over and repositioned the ice before I even realized it was starting to fall off. "You fell like a pro though. The trick is to tuck your chin down, bend your arms at the elbows, and try to land on your side. And to stay relaxed. You're much more likely to get hurt if you're tense."

"Ha," I said. "That's the first time anyone has ever accused me of not getting hurt because I was relaxed." I took a bite of baby greens mixed with thinly sliced pear and goat cheese, and sprinkled with balsamic vinaigrette. "Mmm, this is delicious."

Billy broke off another piece of bread. "Isn't this restaurant great? It's like being in another place and time."

I looked past the herb garden to the fountain in the center of the patio to the perfectly aged stucco walls surrounding us. "They did a great job with all the stonework. It looks like a country cottage somewhere in Europe."

"I've always wanted to go rent one for a month. Maybe in England or France or something."

I nodded. "I know. In France the cottages are called *gîtes*, and there are lots of them on all these picturesque little side streets. I've always dreamed of renting one, too, maybe in Giverny."

Billy took a sip of his iced coffee. "So, where do things stand between you and your ex?"

"You mean, besides the fact that he's not technically my ex?"

"You're not divorced?"

I took a slow sip of my iced tea. "Not to my knowledge," I said.

Billy tilted his head. "That tends to be something one knows about."

When I put my glass back down on the wrought iron table, it tilted sideways. I grabbed for it. My ice fell off. I bent down to pick it up.

I just missed crashing heads with Billy.

"Sorry," I said. I picked up the napkin-wrapped ice and placed it on my knee again.

He leaned back in his chair. "Wow," he said. "You're fairly dangerous."

"That's an understatement," I said.

We looked at each other.

"Here's the thing," Billy said. "If you can work things out with your husband, what's not to like? Nothing beats keeping one big happy original family intact."

"Yeah," I said, "except for the fact that he abandoned us. How could I ever really forgive that? And, I mean, every time he's five minutes late, I'm going to think he's gone again."

Billy shrugged. "People work through a lot of stuff."

I tried to read his eyes through his sunglasses. "Are you trying to get rid of me?"

He laughed. "No. It's just that one thing I've learned is you can't want someone enough for both of you. You'll get back with your husband or you won't. Keep me posted. I mean, what else is there to say?"

The more he talked, the more I didn't want to lose him. "But what are you going to do in the meantime?"

We waited while the waiter took our salads and delivered our salmon. We were so compatible we'd even ordered the same entrée.

"Thanks," Billy said to the waiter. He picked up his fork. "Just keep on keepin' on, I guess. The way I look at it, life's a marathon and not a sprint."

"God," I said. "You're so well adjusted." I was actually starting to think it was a tiny bit irritating.

Billy finished chewing a bite of salmon, then wiped his mouth with his napkin. He even had good table manners. "I just don't need the drama, that's all." A shadow of hurt crossed his face. "My ex-wife fed on drama. Everything was always a big scene."

"That must have been tough."

We ate quietly for a while, thinking our separate thoughts.

"Did you ever sleep with her?" I blurted out. "You know, after you were separated?"

He shrugged. Then he lifted one eyebrow.

"Oh, I'm so relieved," I said. "I thought there was something seriously wrong with me. The whole thing just came out of nowhere."

"It happens," he said.

"It was like what was between Seth and me didn't have anything to do with the rest of the world."

Billy shrugged. "You had your own little world for a lot of years."

"Yeah, I guess."

His eyes met mine. "And sometimes it seems safer to slide backward than to move forward."

"Was it, I mean, did you like sleeping with your ex?"

He reached for his water glass. "If all it took was good sex, a marriage would be a lot easier to keep together," he said finally. "I think eventually it comes down to choosing the life you want, and the person you want to share it with. I don't think it's a choice you can take lightly."

"Clearly, I'm not the best judge of these things," I said. "I thought my husband and I had it all."

Billy picked up his fork. "Maybe you did."

"I don't know. Looking back, he was kind of immature, and maybe a little bit too idealistic."

"Ha. I can remember saying I'd starve before I went into the family business. A few years later, spending my day with bikes was looking pretty good."

I swallowed a bite of perfectly cooked mustard-coated salmon. It felt good to have someone to talk to. I fished a slice of lemon out of my water with a spoon and squeezed it against the side of my glass. "I'm not sure what he's doing since he came back. It's a tough economy, so my guess is he grabbed the first job he found that would give him a steady paycheck. I think eventually most of us get to that point. If you ever told me I'd end up answering phone calls for a travel agency and teaching cooking classes at a community center, I never would have believed you."

28

BILLY HELD THE TRUCK DOOR OPEN FOR ME AND PUT HIS hand under my elbow. "Can you make it?" he asked.

I turned to face him and stepped up with the heel of my good foot to sit sideways on the edge of the long leather seat. I took a moment to bend and straighten my knee a few times. "It actually feels pretty good," I said.

"RICE right away usually does it," Billy said.

"Huh?" I said.

"*R*est, *i*ce, *c*ompression, and *e*levation."

"Wow," I said. "You really know your stuff."

He shrugged. "I've logged a lot of long, hard hours in the bike biz."

I opened my eyes wide. "Right," I said. "Late morning bike rides, leisurely lunches in courtyard cafés . . . Sounds like the life to me."

He grinned. "Especially if you factor out getting up at four-thirty so I could finish what I had to do first. But, yeah, it's a nice life, no question about that."

He looked at his watch, then held out his wrist to me. "How're you doing for time?"

"Fine," I said. "I'll beat the bus with minutes to spare." I put my hand on his forearm. "Thanks for the great lunch. And company."

We looked at each other. He leaned down to kiss me on the cheek.

I turned my head.

"Shit," I said when we finished kissing. I wasn't sure if I meant *shit* that I couldn't keep kissing Billy all day or *shit* that I could feel my life getting complicated.

"Don't blame me," he said. He traced one finger along my cheek, then reached down and lifted my legs into the truck. It was a chivalrous gesture somehow, maybe a suggestion of being carried over some distant threshold.

I hoped he was busy enough closing my door that he didn't hear me sigh.

Billy was quiet as we drove along the pretty, tree-lined streets. I was quiet, too, because I was concentrating on trying not to think. I mean, what was the point? Whatever happened would happen, and in the meantime, the best thing to do was to stay in the moment. Or maybe to drift back just a little, to the moment before the moment, so I could relive that kiss. If only I could freeze time right there, knowing I could go back and push Play again whenever I was ready.

As we turned onto my street, I saw Seth's car in my driveway. My heart started beating like crazy. I was pretty sure I actually gulped.

My mind raced, trying to catch up with my heart. I wondered if I could get away with asking Billy to stop and drop me off right here. Maybe I could say I needed to walk off my lunch, or give my knee a post-RICE workout.

It was a really short street. "Um," I said.

Billy pulled into my driveway. Seth was leaning over my new railings. He looked up. He was holding a paintbrush and a can of paint.

Billy put the truck into park.

"Wow," I said. "What a coincidence. My ex—"

Billy opened the truck door.

"It's okay," I said quickly. "I can let myself out."

He pushed the door open and climbed out. Seth placed the brush in the paint can and put it down on the ground. He wiped his hands on his jeans. I closed my eyes.

When I opened them, Billy and Seth were shaking hands. Then they went in for a guy hug, still holding the handshake but coming together for a quick mutual pat on the back. The shake made sense, but the guy hug seemed awfully civilized, given the circumstances.

But wait.

What *were* the circumstances? For all Billy knew, Seth was just the painter. I mean, how many guys go right up and hug the painter?

There didn't seem to be a choice, so I opened my door and climbed out. My knee didn't really hurt anymore, but I had to fight the urge to limp anyway, like a wild animal who knows that if it acts injured, it might stand a better chance of surviving an attack.

Seth turned to me with a big smile on his face. Billy's face was a little bit harder to read.

"What a small world," Seth said.

"How small?" I said.

"You know that go-between I was telling you about?" Billy said.

I looked at Seth. I looked at Billy.

"No," I said.

"Yeah," Seth said. "Isn't it great? I've started consulting for a few companies, including one of the fair trade companies I dealt with from West Africa, but wow, the chance to go to Japan again is pretty amazing. How do you two know each other anyway?"

It was immature. It was beneath me. I did it anyway.

"I hate you both," I said. And then I limped my way into the house.

HERE'S THE THING ABOUT LIFE: men have all the breaks. I spend the last seven years trying to be a good mom, and where does it get me? Home. Home while my ex-husband, who was probably technically not even an ex, and my possible boyfriend-to-be go away together. Home with my daughter, who even though I loved her more than life itself, would spend the whole time they were off gallivanting around Japan wishing her father was here and I wasn't.

What gave Seth the right to waltz right in, spend a little time with Anastasia and me, then abandon us again to jet off to Japan? It was an easy answer: he was a penis-carrying member of the official worldwide male club, and the perks meant he got all the travel I longed for.

I tried to picture Seth and Billy spending, what, ten days together? Bonding while sharing stories about me over a few drinks. I shivered at the thought. After comparing notes, they'd turn into best friends, and here I'd sit, odd woman out.

I must have dozed off after I finished crying, because a knock on the door jolted me awake.

"Mom?" Anastasia's voice said from the other side of the door.

"Hi, honey," I said in a fake cheery voice.

"Dad wants to know if you want to come out and have some dinner."

"No thanks," I said, as if this were a perfectly ordinary situation. "I had a late lunch."

There was silence on the other side of the door.

"I'm just going to read for a while, honey, and give you some time to hang out with your dad, okay?"

The doorknob turned. I wiggled into a sitting position and fluffed up my hair fast. I hoped my eyes weren't so puffy they'd scare Anastasia.

She poked her head in and reached up to adjust her pink headband. "You don't have a book," she said. "Or a magazine."

"I was just trying to decide what to read. How was school?"

"Okay. Matthew gave Mitchell a black eye so we only got a short recess."

"Men," I said.

Anastasia reached for her headband again. "What?"

"Nothing." I pulled a pillow out from behind me and hugged it. "Sorry I didn't meet your bus today, honey."

"That's okay. Dad was there." Anastasia started disappearing back into the hallway.

"What's for dinner?" I asked, just to keep her there a little longer.

Her head came back in and her hazel eyes met mine. "Sushi. Dad's going to Japan, so we're practicing. He's going to bring me video games and some Japanese T-shirts. And next time he says I can go with him."

I patted the bed beside me. "Sit for a minute."

"I can't," Anastasia said. "I have to go check on my new hamster."

"What?" I said, but my daughter was already gone.

I followed her out to the kitchen. My entire body was getting stiffer by the minute, but I was too furious to care.

Seth was rolling rice, shredded carrots, and cucumber slices into rectangles of seaweed at my kitchen counter. "Hey," he said, without quite looking up.

"You bought her a hamster without discussing it with me first?" I said.

"He's allowed to do that," Anastasia said.

Seth kept rolling.

"Her name is Cammy," Anastasia said. "I'll take care of her. You won't have to do anything."

"She wanted a cat," Seth finally said. "This was a compromise."

I willed my stiff knees to bend and aimed my sore butt at one of the kitchen chairs. "Sit," I said once I'd landed.

They sat.

I crossed my arms over my chest.

"Okay, here's the thing. From now on, any decision that impacts all three of us is first discussed by the two grown-ups in the family."

I looked at Seth. "That would be us."

"But—" Anastasia said.

"Wait," I said. "Any decision—cell phones, hamsters, dates, nose rings, tattoos . . ."

"I can get a tattoo?" Anastasia asked. "When?"

Seth started to open his mouth, but I was faster. "And then, if and only if the grown-ups agree, you'll be brought into the negotiations." I crossed my arms over my chest. "Shall we give it a test run?"

Seth and Anastasia looked like two peas in a pod when they shrugged.

I looked at Seth. "Tattoo. How would you feel about our daughter getting a tattoo?"

"Not a chance in France," Seth said.

"I agree," I said. "End of discussion."

"That's not fair," Anastasia said.

"Life's not fair," I said. "Try us again in a couple of years."

I looked at Seth. "I'd like you to move in for about a week to stay with our daughter so I can go somewhere."

"Okay," Seth said.

I turned to Anastasia. "How would you feel about that?"

"Good," Anastasia said.

"Great," I said. I pushed myself back up to a standing position. "I'll get back to you both with some dates."

As soon as I hobbled back to my bedroom, I picked up my cell phone and called my boss, Joni. "It's Jill," I said. "I'm just wondering. Is it too late to get in on that Costa Rica surfing trip?"

29

MAYBE I HADN'T DONE A LOT OF SMART THINGS IN MY life, but at least I'd renewed my passport last year. It had actually been a birthday present I'd given to myself.

Joni always came through with a gift on my birthday—a book of movie passes or a gift certificate to a restaurant. But for years my only other birthday present had been whatever Anastasia made for me, usually a painting that dried while we baked my birthday cake.

As much as I certainly didn't have money to burn, things were starting to get incrementally easier. I could almost believe that over the course of the next ten years, the life of the passport, I might actually get ahead enough to be able to afford to go somewhere. And somehow I thought if I renewed the passport, maybe it would symbolically pave the way for a trip.

I'd planned on getting Anastasia her first passport at the same time, even if it meant scrimping on groceries for a few weeks. I simply couldn't imagine going anywhere without her. I went online to see if we needed to bring anything besides her birth certificate for documentation. Apparently there was just one small thing: her father. In order to receive a U.S. passport, a child under the age of sixteen had to appear with both parents and sign a form in front of an Acceptance Agent. Those two capital *A*s read like a warning: an Acceptance Agent would be taller and more threatening than a mere acceptance agent, the implication being *don't even think about trying any funny stuff.*

I couldn't be the only single mother in the United States who wasn't able to produce her husband. I scrolled down. Sure enough, I could do this alone. I just had to get Seth to give us a signed and notarized Statement of Consent to take with us. Piece of cake—all I had to do was find him.

I kept reading until I came to Form DS-3053, STATE-MENT OF SPECIAL CIRCUMSTANCES, *to be completed by applying parent or guardian when the written consent of the nonapplying parent or guardian cannot be obtained.*

Use back of form if additional space is needed, it said.

Ha. Not only was the back of the form not nearly spacious enough, even when combined with the front of the form, but all I could see was the big can of worms it would open. *Have you attempted to contact the nonapplying parent or guardian through his parents or other relatives?* the Acceptance Agent would probably ask. *Have you tried to locate him through his employer?*

Form DS-3053 made me consider skipping the birthday travel symbolism and taking a nap instead. But I forced myself to fork over the money to renew at least my passport. Maybe I'd just keep renewing it until Anastasia was old enough to sign for her own passport, and *then* we'd go somewhere together.

A year later, here I sat, on my front steps, amazed and a little bit overwhelmed that I not only had a current passport when I needed one, but it looked like I was actually going to use it before the week was out.

I waved to Anastasia as she lined up with the other kids to get on the bus. She waved back, then pushed some buttons on her Purple People Reacher Phone.

My cell phone rang. I ignored it.

Anastasia gave her head a shake and pointed at her phone.

I pushed a button on my cell. "Sorry," I said. "I didn't think it was you."

"Mom, don't forget to make sure Cammy has plenty of water while I'm at school. I don't know how fast she drinks yet. And make sure you call her Cammy and not anything else, so she doesn't get confused while she's still learning her name. And if you have any questions, just look them up in the hamster book Dad bought me. I have to go, bye."

Anastasia disappeared onto the school bus.

Cynthia sauntered over and plopped down next to me on the steps.

"Hey," I said. "Would you mind being my backup? My ex is going to watch Anastasia while I take a trip to Costa Rica, and I just want to make sure he has an emergency number."

Cynthia leaned back in her tennis outfit and crossed one perfectly formed thigh over the other. My own thighs had been screaming with pain since I woke up this morning. I wondered if they'd ever be crossable again.

"Cheez Whiz," Cynthia said. "Why can't I be single?"

I pulled the T-shirt I'd slept in down over the knees of my baggy gray sweatpants. "Trust me," I said. "It's not as glamorous as it looks."

"You know, I've always wanted to go to Costa Rica," Cynthia said. "Where is it again, girlfriend?"

THE WEEK FLEW BY in a blur of preparations. I picked up extra phone shifts, trading for coverage while I was away, which essentially meant I was tethered to my headphone pretty much round-the-clock. I called everybody in Lunch Around the

World, canceling Monday's class and tacking on an extra class at the end of the session.

They were ridiculously happy for me. "It's about time you had a little fun, a young girl your age," T-shirt Tom said. "You only go around once, you know, honey."

"Don't you worry about us," Ethel said. "We'll still be here when you get back. At least the ones that don't keel over in the meantime. Have you worked things out with the boyfriend yet? Not that I make a point of sticking my nose in where it's not my business, but he seemed like a real sweetheart."

I communicated most of the details of my trip to Seth via Anastasia and her Purple People Reacher Phone. I tried not to think about the fact that it was only a matter of time before we became the subject of one of her spelling sentences. *Dysfunctional*, she'd write. My parents have this *dysfunctional* way of talking to each other through me. *Dysfunctional*.

The rest of the information I wrote down on an ongoing note on a bright yellow legal pad. I left it on the kitchen counter and kept adding things as I thought of them.

—A. hasn't had an ear infection since she was 4½, but if she does, remind the pediatrician that Amoxicillin never works, and to go right to the Augmentin, unless they've come up with a better antibiotic since her last ear infection. Pediatrician's number is on the emergency list, but here it is again, in case the emergency list falls off the refrigerator.

—Make sure A. leaves that cell phone in the kitchen at night, and keeps it turned off whenever possible, since school's still out on the cumulative dangers of electromagnetic radiation.

—Please remember to turn off lights when not in use.

—Sometimes the toilet handle needs to be jiggled to stop the water from running. If you find yourself with extra time on your hands, maybe you could figure out why.

—The computer is off-limits until all homework is done. And please supervise A. when she is on it so she doesn't inadvertently come into contact with the many unsavory characters in cyberspace who prey on innocent young girls.

—Do not let kids next door snack here. Food is far better at their house. Key is under the mat. Good luck finding fridge.

—A. needs her sleep, so do not allow yourself to be manipulated into a later bedtime.

The next time I picked up the yellow legal pad, I saw that Anastasia had crossed out this last entry. Over it she'd written in purple pen: *A. does not need much sleep. Let her stay up as late as she wants.*

Billy called a couple times. Once I was home. I stood in my kitchen and watched his name light up my caller ID, but I didn't pick up. He left messages asking me to call him back, saying he'd like to talk. I thought about it, but what was there to say? We were at such different places in our lives, and with my luck, dating him would only mean I'd be watching his kids, too, while he and Seth ran off to Japan together. It was just the way of the world.

I avoided talking directly with Seth. I mean, what was the point? Every time I thought of him, my chest tightened with resentment. He probably thought he was father of the century for spending a few paltry nights taking care of his daughter, even though he'd shirked that responsibility for most of her life.

And as soon as I got back, he'd head off to Japan for the first of what were sure to be many trips ahead. I'd never really be able to count on him, and the sooner I faced that cold, hard truth, the better off I would be.

I also did my best to avoid Anastasia's new hamster. I told myself it was because I needed to step back so Anastasia would step up and assume full caretaking responsibility. If I changed the cedar shavings or the water bottle, or filled the little food dish, even a single time, it would become my job as soon as the novelty of owning a hamster wore off.

But the truth was, even though it called out to me every time I walked by, I just couldn't let myself get anywhere near that little wire cage with its brightly colored maze of tubes crisscrossing inside like a jungle gym. I had to think of it as an *it* and not a *she*, as *the hamster* and not *Cammy*.

When we were curled up on the couch watching TV after dinner and homework, Anastasia would bring the cage out to sit on our coffee table trunk. She'd reach in and take the hamster out for a cuddle. "Here, Mom," she'd say. "Feel how soft Cammy's fur is."

I'd give it a quick pat with one forefinger, careful not to feel a thing. The last thing I needed was something else that needed me to take care of it.

If I let this little fur ball in, even for a second, it would be all over. Before I knew it I'd be worrying about whether it was getting enough human attention, if it needed another hamster for rodent companionship. Then I'd start waking up in the middle of the night wondering whether I should call the vet to double-check the best ratio of dry food to fresh vegetables, and perhaps discuss the possibility of adding vitamins to its little hamster diet while I had them on the phone. Oh, and should we consider upgrading to a better brand of cedar shavings to risk damaging its delicate little hamster lungs?

The downward spiral would continue. I'd spend hours reworking the plastic tubes into ever more challenging mazes to stimulate its tiny hamster brain. I'd sit at my sewing machine for hours making matching dresses for Cammy and Anastasia. I'd surf the Internet, thinking surely someone must make a pink plastic headband for hamsters.

All over the world, approximately every five seconds, another perfectly intelligent woman gets sucked in like this, the victim of maternal instincts or female hormones, or maybe just a heart that keeps overruling her head.

Each time I passed the hamster cage, that old commercial would play in my mind. *Calgon, take us away,* I wished for us all.

30

THE PLAN WAS TO MEET UP WITH THE GROUP AT THE Miami airport and fly together to San José, Costa Rica. We'd arrive at the San José airport in the early evening, take a chartered bus into the city, have dinner together, and stay the night in a hotel. In the morning we'd wander around, shop, visit a few of the sights, then catch a third plane to our final surfing destination of Tamarindo.

Just before we stepped onto the moving sidewalk between the Logan Airport garage and our terminal, Cynthia and I stopped so she could rearrange her mountains of matching luggage. The Beatles rained down from the sound system, singing "Ticket to Ride" for all they were worth. A shiver ran up my spine as I watched the intricate movements of busy planes through the huge expanse of glass.

This was it. Finally, after all these years, I had my own ticket to ride again. I closed my eyes to take in the enormity of the moment.

Cynthia took off her wide-brimmed straw hat and placed it upside down on one of her suitcases. She rearranged her bangs on her forehead, then spread her arms wide. "We've got a ticket to rye, eye, eyed," she sang. Loudly.

I shook my head. I couldn't believe she'd talked me into letting her come along.

"Shh," I whispered.

A woman walked over and placed a dollar in Cynthia's hat.

"Thanks," Cynthia said. She reached in and handed it to me.

"Keep singing," I said.

"Why?" she said. "I have plastic."

Cynthia and I sat next to each other on the flight from Boston to Miami. The flight attendant offered us the choice of a small packet of honey-roasted nuts—or nothing.

I left my nuts sitting on the tiny tray table in front of me, and took another sip of my ginger ale. My stomach had been tied up in knots since leaving the house this morning.

Seth had arrived early to move his stuff in and get Anastasia on the bus. Anastasia couldn't wait to get me out the door. "Have fun!" she yelled as I got ready to drive off with Cynthia. "Have fun and bring Cammy and me something good. And Dad. Don't forget a present for Dad."

She gave me a hug and a kiss and ran off to give the hamster one more check before school.

I turned to Seth. "Call me if you need to know anything. There's a roaming charge for Costa Rica, so if it's not important, you should e-mail. I'll try to check my e-mail at least twice a day. But if it's the least bit important, just call."

Seth bent down to pick up my bags. With three flights each way, I knew better than to check luggage. I'd managed to cram everything I needed into a big shoulder bag and a rolling carry-on I'd borrowed from Cynthia's family's vast collection, since the last time I'd traveled, rolling suitcases probably hadn't even been invented.

"That's okay," I said. "I can get it myself."

He put my bags back down on the kitchen floor.

I leaned down to grab the handles.

When I stood up, he kissed me on the forehead. "Listen," he said.

"Don't," I said. I looked away from the hurt in his eyes.

He ran his hand through his hair, which was sticking up on the side he'd slept on. "Jill, just tell me. Why are you doing this? I mean, I get that it was probably too much too fast, and I know you really need this trip, but—"

I put my luggage down again. "Here's the thing, Seth. You just got back. You don't *get* anything. And even if you think you do, you don't really know anything about me anymore." Then I ran to find Anastasia to say one more quick good-bye.

Cynthia reached for my honey-roasted nuts. "Can I have these, girlfriend? All I had for breakfast was a handful of Pepperidge Farm croutons."

I turned to look at her.

She was already opening my nuts. "They were almost past their inspiration date. Don't worry, I know it's really expiration. But, I mean, who has time to wash lettuce?"

Are we there yet? I thought. It was going to be a long trip. I closed my eyes and let Cynthia's chatter flow in one ear and out the other, like waves breaking over a pristine beach. I visualized myself standing up on my surfboard on the very first try.

"I am so going to hang ten," I said.

Cynthia crumpled up the empty peanut wrapper and put it back on my tray table. "Fine," she said. "Then I'll hang eleven."

I didn't think women like Cynthia had smaller brains at birth. Their brains probably started out the same size as the rest of ours but withered on the vine while other things, like looks and tennis skills, were being nurtured. Cynthia just needed a good role model. I certainly wasn't going to spend my whole trip being her Henry Higgins, but I thought I could give her some quick coaching that might help her present herself a bit more intelligently to the world.

Sometimes Anastasia would ask me if she was prettier than a classmate at school or even one of the tween flavors-of-the-month at the box office. "You're exactly pretty enough," I'd say, "and how great that you're also smart and creative and kind and funny."

My ten-year-old daughter would let out an impatient puff of air as I launched into a lecture about what a looksist society we were, and how even if there was no denying that a certain amount of attractiveness might make life easier, everyone's beauty fades eventually, and what happens if superficial things like the way you look are the entire basis for your self-esteem.

"Never mind," she'd say when I paused for a breath. "I was only asking who was prettier, me or Emily. I think I am."

I checked my watch. Anastasia was safely in school, and our flight was on schedule. I'd call Seth as soon as we landed in Miami to make sure he'd be on time to meet the bus. If not, I'd have Cynthia call her house and see if whoever was meeting her kids could watch Anastasia until Seth arrived. Tomorrow was Saturday. The weekend would be easier, and by Monday, they'd have the rhythm down. Everything would be fine.

Anastasia could handle this. I could handle this. Even though the pain in my stomach felt like an invisible umbilical cord was being stretched tighter the farther my daughter and I got from each other, Anastasia and I would both be fine. I closed my eyes. "Fine, fine," I whispered to myself slowly, like a mantra.

I turned to Cynthia. "Hang ten is a surfing expression. There is no hang eleven."

Cynthia looked up at the ceiling. "It was a joke. And please tell me you've bought at least one new bathing suit in the last five years."

I ignored her. I'd dug out my ancient bathing suit earlier in the week, and when I gave it a little pull, instead of bouncing back, the tired elastic just gave up and stayed where it was. So I'd been forced to splurge on a simple black tank before I'd left. Even though it was on clearance, I was pretty sure it had to have originated sometime during the last five or so years.

I leaned forward and slid my bag out far enough to get at the plastic folder filled with the tour information Joni had given me. The Costa Rican translator/guide GGG worked with would be doing the heavy lifting, but the more I could help, the better I'd feel about Joni managing to find me a place on the surfing trip at the last minute. I hoped she hadn't bumped anyone to get me this gig, though in my defense, at least I was bringing a paying customer with me, and at great sacrifice to my own personal sanity.

I pulled a pile of computer printouts out of the folder and started flipping through them. Cynthia recrossed her legs in their tight white capris and started talking to a guy in a business suit, who seemed to be doing his best not to drool.

Costa Rica, the first sheet said, is roughly the size of Vermont or West Virginia. There are over six hundred species of butterflies, and almost ten thousand species of plants, including thousands of orchids. I couldn't wait to see the orchids.

Temperatures in Costa Rica ranged between eighty and a hundred degrees year-round, and we'd be arriving at the beginning of the rainy season, when it tended to stay sunny until late afternoon. Showers built inland and moved offshore, producing spectacular sunsets. Sounded good to me. The Pacific coast area, where Tamarindo was located, tended to be drier and sunnier, as well as windier.

I skimmed down. There are no street addresses or building numbers in Costa Rica. For landmarks, one used other buildings or even trees. This, and the fact that my Spanish consisted of *por favor* and *gracias*, made me glad I was going to essentially be just another set of hands.

Cynthia laughed throatily beside me. "My *husband* always says I dress to kill and cook the same way," she said. She shifted toward me. I ignored her.

She elbowed me. I looked up.

Cynthia turned in her seat, flipped her hair, and pointed over her shoulder. "Pig," she mouthed.

"Then stop flipping your hair," I said, maybe a little too loudly.

Cynthia scratched her cheek with her middle finger. "It's a free airplane. I can flip whatever I want."

I ignored her and went back to reading. Costa Rican natives called themselves *Tico*, by which they meant friendly, laid-back, helpful, educated, and environmentally aware.

"What are you reading about?" Cynthia chirped.

I closed my eyes. "Alaska," I said.

"Ha," Cynthia said. She leaned over my shoulder. "Okay, tell me something I don't know about Costa Rica."

I took a deep breath and tried to channel my inner *Tico*.

I ruffled through my papers. "Let's see," I said. "Costa Rica is a tiny country nestled between North and South America."

"Doesn't it have to choose one?"

"Actually," I said, "it's in Central America."

"Wow, you'd make a great geometry teacher."

"Why do you do that?" I asked.

Cynthia opened her eyes wide. "What?"

"Pretend to be stupid."

"I don't know, I guess because it helps me get away with more. Okay, now tell me about the shopping."

"Well, tomorrow we'll hit the outdoor markets in San José. Bartering is the accepted practice—it's actually expected. It says here we should try to settle at about eighty percent of the original asking price."

Cynthia held up her hand for a high five. "Stick with me, girlfriend, and you'll be fine. I haven't paid retail since whoever was president before that last guy."

31

I'D FORGOTTEN HOW MUCH I LOVED AIRPORTS. ESPE-
cially at the beginning of trips, when all your clothes are clean
and neatly packed, and everything seems possible. Seth and I
had spent many a happy day or night, sometimes both, waiting for a cheap standby fare to materialize into an actual flight.
We'd flip through magazines, browse the duty-free shops, share
a bottle of water, people-watch to our hearts' content.

The cheap standby fares were long gone, and bottled water
now cost an arm and a leg. This was the first time I'd flown post-
9/11, and even though I'd watched plenty of airport security
news coverage, I'd still been a little bit overwhelmed when I
went through security at Logan. I'd flashed back to a long-ago
trip to Amsterdam, when Seth and I were separated and inter-
rogated about our visit by separate security guards. Even though
we weren't carrying anything illegal, I was sure we were going
to be arrested for *something*.

I'd felt the same wave of guilt at Logan as a TSA official
fingered my Ziploc bag with her latex-gloved hand. I'd guzzled
the last of my water and thrown away the bottle, but could the
mascara in the bottom of my carry-on possibly be considered a
liquid? How about my allegedly solid deodorant?

Cynthia had checked her luggage back in Boston. She
walked ahead of me in her ridiculous straw hat, her little pais-
ley Vera Bradley bag swung perkily from one shoulder while

I tried to balance my shoulder bag on the carry-on I was rolling.

It was hard to believe I was actually going somewhere. For almost a decade, all my trips had been imaginary. I downloaded Google Earth as soon as I heard about it, and I'd spent many a happy hour looking at satellite photos of the Cornish coast, taking the Art Nouveau tour of Brussels, enjoying the geosights of Utah. Long before that, I'd salvaged old issues of *National Geographic Traveler, Condé Nast Traveler,* and *Travel + Leisure* from the GGG offices, taking them home and flipping through them ravenously, night after night.

New online travel magazines for women seemed to pop up almost weekly, and I bookmarked as many as I could find: journeywoman.com, tangodiva.com, gogalavanting.com, travel girlinc.com, womenstravelmagazine.com, womensadventure magazine.com, wanderlustandlipstick.com. I binged on them all, like a foodaholic who'd never met a box of cookies that didn't call out to her.

Miami International Airport lived up to its name, since it bustled with people from all over the world. Lots of them seemed to be speaking Spanish, but I also caught bits and pieces in German and French and Chinese, and what I thought might have been Brazilian Portuguese.

I caught up to Cynthia at the departure screen. "God Bless America is what I say," a woman with a thick accent I couldn't identify yelled. "Bless them and have mercy on them all at the same time."

"Wow," Cynthia said. "I guess she likes it here already."

Two big guys in TSA uniforms stepped up to either side of the woman and grabbed her arms.

Cynthia looked up at the overhead screen. "San José de Costa Rica," she read. "Is that us?"

"It is indeed," I said. "Great, the plane's on time. And they said it couldn't be done."

I rolled toward our departure terminal on the other end of Terminal D. We were walking past the escalator that went to the lower level.

Cynthia stopped and looked down. She made a movement with her shoulders that was half shiver, half shimmy. "Ooh, how about that little girl who got her foot stuck here? My mother always used to tell me if you want to get your money's worth on your pedicure, Cynthia Paige, keep your toes out of the escalator."

"What?" I said. "What happened?"

Cynthia tried to raise her eyebrows, but nothing moved. "To my mother?"

"No," I said. "The little girl."

"Oh, she was wearing those plastic garden shoes."

I looked down at the sharp metal teeth swelling toward us. "Like the pink ones Anastasia has?"

Cynthia nodded. "I'm not sure what color they were, but apparently escalators gobble those little shoes right up."

I was already calling Seth.

"Listen," I said when he answered. "If you take Anastasia anywhere that has an escalator, make sure she doesn't wear those pink garden shoes of hers. And make sure she stands in the middle of the step and doesn't lean into the handrail. And whatever you do, don't let her sit down." I took a breath. "Maybe you should just avoid escalators altogether and take the elevator. Or use the stairs. Unless it's a soccer day and she's tired."

"Jill, I don't even know where the nearest escalator is. Come on, relax. Everything's going to be fine."

"You have no way of knowing that," I said.

There was a pause. "Okay, I have no way of knowing that. But I'll be on time for her bus, I won't let her stay up too late, and I'll keep her off escalators. Try to have some fun, okay?"

"Okay," I said. "Thanks."

I stopped to put my cell phone back in my shoulder bag, then started rolling again.

Cynthia fell into step beside me. Her phone rang.

It kept ringing.

"Aren't you going to answer that?" I said.

"No way," she said. "I'm in my perfect window of relaxation."

I scanned the restaurants we passed. "We should definitely try to get some Cuban food if we can," I said.

Cynthia's phone rang again. She unlooped her Vera Bradley bag from her shoulder and fished out her phone. She pushed a button and the ringing stopped.

A moment later her phone rang again.

I stopped walking. "Answer that," I said. "Or I will."

Cynthia held the phone out in my direction. I shook my head. I crossed my arms over my chest.

"Hi there," she finally said in a singsongy, little girl voice. "Mm-hmm. Mm-hmm. I bet, baby. Listen, the plane is about to take off, so I have to hang up now. Okay, okay. Wait a minute."

She took the cell away from her ear. "What's your ex's number? Deck needs him to get our three off the bus, too."

It seemed only fair that Seth got a true taste of my world, so I gave it to her. I didn't even feel guilty.

My stomach growled. I went back to scanning the terminal restaurants for possibilities. "Ooh, La Carretta," I said.

We made our way over to the take-out line. "What's your most popular sandwich?" I asked the man behind the register.

"The Elena Ruz," he said.

"Does it come with plaintain chips?" Cynthia asked.

He nodded.

"What are they?" Cynthia asked.

I looked up at the clock over the register. They'd be boarding our plane any minute. "We'll take two," I said.

Cynthia didn't immediately reach for her money, so I held out my hand until she went for her wallet. I'd learned this way back in my college days, when the richest girl in my dorm kept hitting me up for quarters to do her laundry and never once paid me back. If I ran into her today, it would be all I could do not to ask for my $3.75 back. I'd worked hard for my money, even back then, racking up as many boring hours as my federal work study grant would allow each semester.

"Plaintains," I said as we hurried to our gate, "are actually in the banana family, but they're cooked instead of eaten raw. A fully ripened plaintain tastes like a cross between a banana and a sweet potato, and plaintain chips taste just like sweet potato chips. Plaintains are very popular in Cuba, as are malangas, which are also a lot like sweet potatoes, and boniatos, which are similar to sweet potatoes, only they're white."

"Thanks," Cynthia said. "But some of us just like to eat our food."

I saw a green triangular flag that read GREAT GIRLFRIEND GETAWAYS surrounded by a group of women. And then I saw Joni.

I sprinted over and gave her a big hug and a kiss. "I can't believe you're here!"

She ran one hand through her coarse gray hair. "I just thought, what the hell, I might as well enjoy the perks as long as I own the business. And I haven't been to Costa Rica in ages. I hope it's not one big parking lot yet. Come on, you two, let me introduce you to the group."

The group turned out to be a mixed bag. Mostly midlife, about half of them traveling solo. Three old high school friends, a couple of sorority sisters, a freelance journalist, some real surf enthusiasts who let the rest of us know they even traveled with their own boards, an attorney, a recent divorcée who was already telling everybody about her divorce, some retirees. A few

younger women were in the group, too. They were fully en-
gaged with texting, and the expressions on their faces were
skeptical, as if they thought they might have picked the wrong
trip.

There was a buzz in the air. Excitement. Expectation. A
little bit of apprehension. It was almost palpable, whirling around
our group and connecting us to one another with a force field of
energy.

Joni did a head count, then rolled the GGG flag around the
little wooden pole.

"What do you need?" I asked.

"Some fun," she said. "And you do, too. How're you holding up so far?"

"Great," I said. "Well, not great, but pre-great."

"Give it time," Joni said.

Cynthia had managed to find a seat and was already working
on her sandwich. I walked over and grabbed mine before she
had a chance to eat it. "Mmm, this is good," she said. "I have no
idea how turkey, cream cheese, and strawberry marmalade got
to be Cuban, but do me a favor, don't illuminate me, okay?"

32

THE FLIGHT ATTENDANTS PASSED OUT THE COSTA RICAN Immigrations/Custom Form for us to fill out during the flight, so when our plane landed at the San José airport two hours, forty-five minutes, and many bumps later, we were ready to head right to customs.

We gathered around Joni for a head count. "If you haven't already done it," she said, "don't forget to change whatever gadgets you're carrying to Central Time. Not that time really matters on this trip, except for meeting up purposes."

A few women reached for their watches or cell phones. The rest of us smiled tentatively at one another. It felt a lot like the first day of summer camp, when you looked around and wondered who would be your friends by the end of the week.

"I'm Joni, and if you haven't met her yet, I'd like you to meet Jill, who's been with Great Girlfriend Getaways for almost seven years."

"Hi, everybody," I said. I thanked Joni silently for not pointing out that I'd been tethered to my headphone the whole time.

Joni nodded at the woman to her right. "This is Vianca. She's been guiding our Costa Rica trip from its inception. If you need to know anything about anything, Vianca will help you find the answer."

Vianca was about my age. She had exotic features and a sleek geometric haircut, and she was wearing jeans and a black tank with a big chunky ethnic necklace. She wasn't beautiful by conventional standards, but she carried herself in such a way that you couldn't take your eyes off her. I wanted to *be* her.

"*¿Qué hubo?* Vianca said. "That pretty much means 'what's up?' Costa Ricans normally say it like *¿Quiubo?* The weakening of the *e* to an *i* at the end of a word is very common in Costa Rican Spanish." She grinned. "Or you can just smile and leave the rest to me."

"Thank you," one of the women said.

"*Gracias*," someone else said.

"Show off," somebody else said.

"Okay," Vianca continued. "There are only eight gates in this airport, so even though we've come in at the farthest gate, it's just a hop, skip, and a jump over to immigration."

Cynthia put her hand up.

Vianca nodded at her.

"Do we have to immigrate?" Cynthia asked.

A couple of women swallowed back laughs, but Vianca looked at her kindly. "Don't worry," she said, "they won't try to keep you here."

"Ha," Cynthia said. "Even if my family begs them to?"

Cynthia got a bigger laugh than I thought she actually deserved. Vianca and Joni led the way, and we all followed the signs, printed in both English and Spanish, toward immigration and baggage.

Vianca turned around and started walking backward, and I had a flashback to one of my own tour guide days, when the dozen or so people in my group let me walk right into a pole. I didn't see anything in Vianca's path, but I kept an eye out for her just in case.

"We're going to walk right past the souvenir shop," Vianca said, "since you can buy the same stuff literally ten times cheaper in downtown San José."

There was a desk just inside the immigration hall.

Save Time on the day of Departure,
buy Your departure tax today.

We all stopped and took a moment to puzzle over the odd capitalization.

"Most countries include this tax in the cost of the airline ticket," Vianca said, "but not Costa Rica."

A couple of women groaned, and we all started to reach for our wallets.

"But Great Girlfriend Getaways has included your departure tax in the cost of the tour," Vianca continued. "So if you'll line up, I'll hand each of you twenty-six dollars in cash."

There was a pleased group murmur, and everybody started filing obediently into a single line. I stepped back to the end with Joni. "Little touches can make a big difference," Joni whispered. "When people look back on a trip, you don't want them to remember being nickeled and dimed to death."

"If you come back again without GGG," Vianca was saying as she handed us each a crisp twenty, a five, and a one-dollar bill, "you should remember to bring cash, to save yourself a steep little service charge for using your ATM. Also, we'll wait till we get to a bank in San José to change your dollars into colones, since we'll get the best rate there."

Vianca herded us over to the tourist line. An enormous photo mural of people riding ziplines through the lush Costa Rican tropical rain forest kept us company while we waited. I wondered if I'd ever have the nerve to try something like that. Surfing seemed a lot less challenging.

We prepaid our departure tax and tucked our receipts away for safekeeping. As I rode the escalator down to the baggage claim, I tried hard not to imagine Anastasia's feet getting caught in its shiny metal teeth. I focused instead on another huge photo mural slanting down over our heads. A waterfall burst out of the lush tropical growth and landed in a pool below. I could almost hear the roar of the water. Enormous white letters proclaimed WELCOME TO COSTA RICA.

I blew out a long gust of air and reminded myself to savor every single detail of this trip. Who knew when I might get the chance to go somewhere again.

About twenty minutes later, everyone but Cynthia had their luggage.

"Don't even tell me," Cynthia said.

Vianca draped an arm over Cynthia's shoulder. "Come on. I'll help you fill out the lost-luggage form. With any luck, they'll deliver your belongings to our hotel before we fly out tomorrow."

"Lost luggage," Cynthia said as she made quotation marks with two fingers of each hand. "Right. How do we know somebody didn't just steal the suitcases with the best clothes?"

"We'll fill out that form, too, while we're over there," Vianca said.

"Don't worry," I said. "You can always borrow some of my clothes."

Cynthia gave my T-shirt and jeans a once-over. "Or we could shop," she said.

AS SOON AS Cynthia and I checked into our bungalow, I made a dash for the business center to check my e-mail. Nothing. I checked my cell phone again. Not a single message.

My eyes filled up. No news is good news, I reminded myself. Anastasia and Seth had lots of catching up to do, and it was perfectly understandable they'd forgotten all about me. It was a good thing, and because of it, I was in San José, Costa Rica, having the time of my life.

A single tear rolled down one cheek. It dead-ended at the corner of my mouth, and I wiped it away with the back of my hand. I opened a blank e-mail and started writing to Anastasia.

Dear Asia,
I hope you're having as much fun with Dad as I am in Costa
Rica! If you have time, I'd love to hear all about your day,
but if you're busy, especially if you're doing your homework,
which I know you won't forget, I completely understand.
Love,
Mom

I reread it. I knew the chances were slim, but if I happened to get eaten by a shark or a crocodile while I was surfing, this was not the letter I'd want my daughter to remember me by. I deleted it and tried again.

Hi Honey!
I'm having a great time in Costa Rica! I miss you oodles,
but know you're having adventures of your own. I can't wait
to hear all about them.

Ugh. What kind of mother misses her daughter *oodles*? I highlighted the whole thing and pressed Delete.

Dear Anastasia,
I love you more than life itself, and as hard as it is for me to
be away from you, even for a night, I know when we both

look back, we'll see this as a significant growth period in
both of our lives.

Yikes. If this e-mail didn't send her straight to therapy, I
didn't know what would. Why was it so ridiculously hard to
write a letter to my own daughter? What was my problem? I
lifted my hands off the keyboard and shook them hard, then
tried again.

Hey Sweetie,
Having a great time! Wish you were here!
Love,
Mom

I pushed Send fast. Then I opened up a blank e-mail for
Seth. I stared at it for a while, thinking of all the things I should
and shouldn't say to him, about Anastasia, about us. Finally I
wrote:

Seth,
Please let me know if this e-mail goes through.
—Jill

33

I STOPPED FOR A MOMENT TO LISTEN TO THE PIANO
player in the lobby, then made my way out to the open-air sidewalk café. Most of the women were already seated at round tables shaded by deep salmon market umbrellas.

"Don't sit next to anyone you already know," Vianca was
saying to two women who'd walked out just ahead of me.

The women rolled their eyes, but they separated. Joni and
Vianca were each at a different table, so I took a seat at the third
table.

We were spending the night at the Gran Hotel Costa Rica,
a 1930s pale salmon and white-trimmed throwback to a
grander time. Not only was it an official national historic land-
mark, but the location was also perfect—according to my notes,
we were surrounded by the pedestrian-only streets of the Plaza
de la Cultura and directly across from Teatro Nacional.

I could still hear the piano music, something jazzy and unidentifiable, through the open windows, and when I looked through
the wrought iron fence at the throngs of people milling past, it almost seemed as if they were walking to the beat of the music. I
couldn't imagine a better place to feel the Latin rhythm of San José.

"Can you believe John F. Kennedy stayed here?" one of the
women at my table said.

I smiled at her. "So cool. And Harry Truman, too."

"Let's not forget Julio Inglesias and John Wayne," one of
the other women said.

Cynthia came out of nowhere and sat down in the chair directly across from me. "Don't you just hate that? I mean, you think you're doing something totally different, and you find out everybody else got here first."

She was wearing my favorite skirt, the one from Anthropologie. Even though I'd bought it on clearance and had had it forever, I'd kill her if she spilled anything on it. She looked down at her new pink gift shop T-shirt. PURA VIDA was splashed across the front of the shirt in optimistic green letters. "I bet everyone probably has a T-shirt like this, too," Cynthia said.

It might not have been unique enough for Cynthia, but *pura vida* was my favorite Costa Rican expression. The direct translation is "pure life," but *pura vida* could also mean everything from "you're good people" to "the good life to you" or "to life." If something was cool or awesome, you could even say it was *pura vida*.

I checked my cell phone one more time to make sure I hadn't somehow missed a message, only to have it pop up with better open-air cell reception.

A tall, dark, and handsome waiter came over and asked for our drink order in English. One of the women ordered *guaro*, which I'd read was similar to a rough and not-so-great Costa Rican vodka.

"No way, José," our waiter said with a look of mock terror.

Even though he probably used this line on all his tables, we cracked up.

"What would you suggest then?" the same woman asked.

"Caipirinhas are the new mojitos!" our waiter said with an adorable wink. I hoped he got a commission on them, because every woman at our table ordered one. A couple of them looked like they'd order up the waiter, too, if they could.

Since I'd done my research, I knew the caipirinha (kai-pur-EEN-ya) and the mojito share two primary ingredients, lime and sugar. The mojito adds rum, mint leaves, and soda water and is served in a tall glass. The caipirinha adds only crushed ice and Cachaça (ka-sha-sa), a Brazilian rum distilled from sugarcane juice, to a lime muddled with two tablespoons of sugar.

"Whew," one of the women said as we tried our first sips. "Those Brazilians sure know their rum. I might have to think about a trip to Brazil next."

"A-okay?" the cute waiter asked, making a little circle with his thumb and index finger, and extending his three remaining fingers.

"A-okay," we all chorused, imitating his gesture.

He winked. "I make my highest effort to comfort your stay," he said. When he walked away, we all turned to follow him with our eyes.

One of the sorority sisters made a swooning sound.

"Well, you can't argue with that," the recently divorced woman said. I was pretty sure her name was Janice. "If my ex had made even his lowest effort to comfort my stay, I might not be spending the money I got divorcing him on this trip."

"Do you think we should ask for menus?" the lawyer said, clearly hoping to redirect Janice before she started talking about her divorce again.

I was glad I'd gone over my trip notes again on the flight to Miami. "An assortment of *bocas* is included in the trip," I said. "*Ticos*, or Costa Ricans, love to snack, and *bocas* are Costa Rican appetizers. GGG has ordered us a *boca* feast fit for a *Tico*. *Gallos*—tortillas piled with meat, chicken, or beans, and cheese; ceviche—a marinated seafood salad; tamales—stuffed cornmeal patties wrapped and steamed inside banana leaves; and *patacones*—fried green plaintain chips."

"Don't get her talking about those," Cynthia said, "or we'll be here all night."

"Don't forget whose skirt you're wearing," I said, as if I were only kidding.

Cynthia took another sip of her caipirinha. "Don't remind me. Does anyone know what time the stores open in the morning?"

"I'm dying to go to the jade museum," somebody said.

"I hear the Teatro Nacional is amazing," somebody else said. "I wish we could see a performance there, but I definitely want to at least take a tour."

"I hope we start with the outdoor market," the sorority sister said.

"All I want to do is surf," one of the surfers said.

A woman leaned forward. "How much did it cost you to bring your surfboard on the plane?"

The surfer shrugged. "A hundred dollars."

"Each way, Michelle?" somebody said to the surfer.

She nodded.

"Couldn't you rent one cheaper than that?" I said.

Michelle shrugged. She was probably in her thirties, long limbed and all angles, like a tomboy who didn't quite know how to grow up. Her sun-bleached hair was frizzy and wild, and her nose was sprinkled with freckles.

Michelle shrugged some more. "It's just not the same. It might sound crazy, but once you get to know your board, I don't know, it's almost like you're looking out for each other. And once you get a bad case of board love—"

"Board love?" somebody said.

"You'd never want to cheat on it?" Janice said. "Oh, puh-lease. Can you imagine a guy worrying about how many boards he rode?"

"I'm so not going to touch that line," somebody said.

Two new cute waiters cut through our laughter to place the first of our *bocas* on the table. I took one more look at my cell phone, then put it away in my shoulder bag.

"Did anybody else have a hard time leaving your kids?" popped out of my mouth.

"Ohmigod," a woman with salt-and-pepper hair said, as she reached for a tamale. "It's the worst. And mine are twenty-eight and thirty-two."

After the laughter died down, a woman who hadn't said anything yet spoke. "There was this robin?" she said.

We all waited.

The woman blushed.

Janice put a *patacone* back on her plate and rested her hand on the woman's. "Go ahead, tell us. Linda, right?"

Linda nodded. She had dark hair and beautiful skin, like the old Pond's cold cream commercials.

"I'm here with my sister," Linda said. "We're both so busy we never see each other, and we used to vacation at the beach when we were kids, so we picked this trip as an excuse to get together. Anyway, at home I've been watching this robin who built a nest outside my bedroom window. You know, kind of tucked into the wisteria snaking up the drainpipe?"

We all nodded encouragingly.

Linda took a breath. "The nest is above eye level, so I couldn't see inside, but I could watch the mother robin sitting on it. One day I noticed fluffy new feathers and tiny beaks peeking over the edge of the nest. Then before I knew it, one of the babies started hanging over the edge, and the mother would have to sit on its head to push it back down into the nest."

"Been there," someone said.

We all laughed.

Linda wrapped both hands around her drink, as if she were trying to keep it safe. "Occasionally another adult bird would stop by to sit next to the mother for a while."

"Probably the father," I said as the caipirinha reached my brain, "swinging by between stints in the Peace Corps."

Fortunately, the caipirinhas must have reached their brains at the same time, because everybody laughed.

"I bet it was just a girlfriend dropping by to chat, or to borrow a cup of worms," the salt-and-pepper-haired woman said.

"Or to see if she wanted to go out cruising for boy birds," Michelle said.

"I hope she had more sense than that," Janice said. "That's what got her stuck in that nest in the first place."

Linda waited until we settled down. "Then right before I left this morning, one of the babies was sitting out on a curled branch of wisteria. Just sitting there, like, bet you can't make me come back to the nest."

Linda's eyes teared up.

"What?" somebody said.

Linda was sobbing quietly now. Janice handed her a tissue, and Linda dabbed her eyes and blew her nose.

"I know this is totally crazy," Linda said. "But I can't stop thinking that when I get back home, they'll all be gone, and I'll never see them again."

Linda blew her nose once more. Somebody else sniffed.

"Okay, it's a little bit crazy," Cynthia said, "but not too bad."

I tried to catch Cynthia's eye, in case making her shut up was even a remote possibility, but she was too busy picking all the shrimp out of the ceviche.

Cynthia bit a shrimp in half. "Birds will come and birds will go," she said as she reached for her caipirinha. "I mean, whatever. But here's the thing: eventually we all have to learn to friend for ourselves."

34

"BINGO," JONI SAID. "LOOKS LIKE YOU FOUND IT."

We were standing outside a stall at the outdoor market on the Plaza de la Democracia. I was going with the plaza's theme by electing to keep my distance from Cynthia, so I wouldn't have to kill her.

When I'd awoken this morning, Cynthia's bed was empty and the bathroom door was open. I poked my head into the tiny bathroom, just in time to see Cynthia aiming my toothpaste-laden toothbrush at her mouth.

"Don't even think about it," I said.

Cynthia turned. "What?"

I grabbed my toothbrush out of her hand.

"It wasn't my first choice either, girlfriend," Cynthia said. "But as long as what's mine is missing, I just figured—"

"What's mine is yours?" I said. "I don't think so."

I waited while Cynthia finger-brushed her teeth, then brushed my own. I pocketed my toothbrush and went down to check my e-mail.

A message from Anastasia's e-mail address popped up right away.

Mom,
Me and Dad and Cammy are doing awesome.
Take your time.

Love,

Asia

P.S. Dad said to tell you the e-mail came thrugh.

I'd printed out a copy of Anastasia's e-mail and tucked it into my purse. I'd already taken it out and reread it twice. I resisted the urge to go for a third time. Instead, I held a little hand-painted oxcart outside the stall, so I could see it better in the bright San José sunlight.

In the next stall, I heard Vianca's rich, melodic voice. "Artisans in Guanacaste make these pieces, which are re-creations of pre-Columbian Chorotega-style pottery. There are some wonderful examples here, and the prices are good. I can help you arrange for shipping, so you don't have to lug them to Tamarindo, if you're so inclined."

"Anastasia will love that one," Joni said.

I was still looking at the oxcart. "I don't know," I said. "It's *almost* pink, but I think it's really more of a red."

Joni pointed. "It's close enough, and look, some of the details are painted in a pale pink."

I tilted the oxcart. "I think that's just the red paint showing through the white."

Oxcarts are an important part of Costa Rican history, since they were traditionally used to transport coffee from Costa Rica's Central Valley to the deep-water ports of Puntarenas. We'd passed bright hand-painted oxcarts big enough to carry a person, and smaller ones that had been made into napkin holders. I'd never admit it in a million years, but part of the draw of the one I was holding was that it was the perfect size to fit a hamster.

I decided the oxcart was close enough to pink. I also couldn't resist a framed, hand-painted feather, another specialty of Costa Rican artisans. It was signed by a local painter who had managed to fit an amazingly realistic and brightly colored hummingbird, a frog, and flowers on a single feather. Anastasia would love it, and I knew she'd want to paint some of her own as soon as she saw it. I'd have to remember to keep my eye out for feathers while we were here.

I added a hand-painted *PURA VIDA* T-shirt in Anastasia's size. My shopping budget was essentially shot for the trip, but I'd have my Costa Rican memories, so it wasn't as if I needed a souvenir for myself.

Some of our group looked on as the stall owner and I bartered away. When we reached the expected 80 percent of the asking price, we both smiled as I handed over my colones.

"If you both know you're supposed to get a discount, why not just lower the price?" one of the women asked as we headed for the next stall.

"It's all part of the game," Joni said. "You don't want to ruin the fun."

"Speaking of fun," I said as Joni and I walked ahead of the others, "don't you think you'll miss all this?"

Joni looked around at the bustling marketplace. "This? I haven't done *this* in years. It's amazing how even the most creative business idea can turn into nothing but bookkeeping and bill paying before you know it. What I'm trying to dig myself out from under are the mountains of paperwork. Maintenance and paperwork."

"What made you start GGG?" I couldn't believe I'd never asked her before.

"Good Lord, it feels like a million years ago." Joni stopped to look at a display of pre-Columbian reproduction jewelry. I recognized the figures as *huacas*, images of ancient deities resembling animals. I knew Panama, Mexico, and Costa Rica each had their regional designs.

Joni picked up a silver and jade frog with splayed feet.

"Aww," I said. "It's so cute. You should definitely treat yourself."

"The last thing I need is more stuff," Joni said. She put the frog pin back down and picked up a pair of bird earrings. "What was the question again?"

I opened my mouth.

"Oh, right," Joni said, before I could say anything. "GGG. I was a young widow, my kids were off on their own, or close to it, and suddenly it occurred to me that I'd been taking care of everybody else my whole life, and now they'd all up and left me."

Before I knew it, Anastasia would be gone, too. My eyes teared up. "Oh, that's so sad."

"I survived," Joni said. "And I mean, it's not like I didn't still see my kids. But suddenly I had hours to fill for the first time I could remember. So I picked a destination and phoned some of my friends in similar situations, simply because I didn't want to travel alone."

"Where did you go?" I asked.

Joni laughed. "New York City. It was as far away as I could dream. But we saw the sights, went to a show on Broadway, shopped, and ate at divine restaurants. And as soon as we got back, my phone was ringing off the hook—old friends who couldn't believe I hadn't thought to invite them and wanted to know when the next trip was."

"And presto," I said. "A business was born."

Joni shook her head. "Hardly. I kept my day job for years and took it one trip at a time. At first we were just a group of women traveling together, then I caught on to getting a group discount to cover my own costs, and finally I took a few courses. Travel was my passion, and the business grew as a by-product of that, almost without my noticing what was happening."

"Wow," I said. "You've come a long way, baby."

"Ha. Sometimes the trick is knowing when to stop. I had a lot more fun when it was a travel club."

"Did you ever meet another man after your husband died?" I asked. Joni rarely talked about her life beyond GGG.

"Sure," Joni said. "A couple of them. And then one day you realize it's not about the guy. That longing in your heart is always going to be there."

"So you just gave up on men?"

"I didn't say that." Joni picked up the pace and wove her way through the crowded Plaza de la Democracia. I followed her crisp gray hair, sparkling like a beacon in the bright sunshine, until I caught up with her. "I've had a rendezvous or two lately."

"Stop," I said. "Match.com?"

"At my age, it would be more like Rematch.com." She shrugged and looked at her watch. Across from us, a group of GGG women were bartering for bottled water as if their lives depended on it.

"What do you say we round up those wild women and head back to the hotel so we don't miss that plane?" Joni said.

35

CYNTHIA'S LUGGAGE HAD SHOWN UP AT THE GRAN HOTEL just in the nick of time. It was hard to tell which one of us was more excited. A porter had wheeled her two gargantuan suitcases out to us just as we were climbing into the vans that would take us to the Pavas Airport in San José.

"*Woo-hoo*," I yelled when I saw the suitcases.

"Whew, that was a clothes call," Cynthia said.

Our group had booked every seat on the small Nature Air plane that was flying us directly into Tamarindo. "If you come back here on your own," Vianca said as we lined up to board, "make sure you get the '*locos*' rate. All the seats are essentially the same, so it's a waste of money to pay for '*elite*' or '*promo*' seats."

The pilot chatted throughout our fifty-minute flight, telling us that the mission of Nature Air, besides being environmentally responsible, was to create memorable experiences for travelers by featuring oversize windows in their fleet of Dash 6 Twin Otters that turned every flight into a sky tour.

It wasn't much of an exaggeration. The pilot pointed out volcanoes and rain forests and waterfalls below us, and the fifty-minute flight was a great way to get a sense of the incredible natural beauty of the country. It also saved us almost five hours of driving over the potholes of Costa Rica's legendary bad roads.

"It's just so green," somebody said.

"In more ways than one," another woman said. "I loved that even the bath products at the hotel were green. What a great country."

"There's much to admire about Costa Rica's concern for the environment," Vianca said behind me. "But as ecotourism has become more of a draw, greenwashing has also become more of a problem. For instance, hotels can receive government sustainable certificates just by using biodegradable cleaning products, recycling, and not using pesticides, even if they're not actively promoting wider conservation efforts."

"Joni Mitchell was so far ahead of her time with those lyrics about paving paradise and putting up a parking lot," I said.

Cynthia turned around in front of me. "Are you sure? I always thought it was pay paradise to put in a parking lot. You know, like everyone was trying to get into paradise, so they needed more parking."

Once again, Cynthia got a bigger laugh than I thought she deserved, especially since I didn't think she even got her own joke. The other women really seemed to like her, possibly more than they liked me. If we were in high school, she'd probably be a cheerleader or a prom queen or something, and far too cool to hang out with me.

Cynthia had finished unloading one of her suitcases and was now working on putting the contents of the other into the remaining drawers of the small dresser we were supposed to be sharing. It didn't really matter, since most of my clothes were dirty at this point anyway.

I was trying to decide whether to wash up before dinner or check my e-mail first.

I watched Cynthia stack an amazing assortment of undergarments in the drawer.

"Wow," I said. "Do you really wear all that stuff?"

"Eventually," she said, "if I live long enough." She held up a long beige thing with a high waist and legs. "I even dream in Spanx. Actually, I'm a Spanx carnivore."

"Now there's an appetizing thought," I said.

Cynthia wiggled in between the two suitcases and plopped down on her bed. "I can do the time line of my life in Spanx. It's fascinating."

"I bet," I said as I backed toward the door.

"No, really." Cynthia reached up to yank her bangs across her forehead. "Okay, in 1998, the owner of Spanx cut off the feet of her panty hose to look smashing in her white pants."

I reached one hand out behind me. I turned the doorknob.

Cynthia jumped up, opened a dresser drawer, and held up a pair of white capris. "I had the exact same idea. And not to be competitive, but I'm almost positive it was sometime in 1997."

She refolded the capris and leaned over to put them back in the drawer. "In 2001, she invented the control-top fishnet and coined the phrase 'no more grid butt.'"

Cynthia spun around and held out both hands, like Vanna White after she'd revealed a particularly good letter. "I'd been wearing bike shorts over my fishnets for at least a year at that point."

The mention of bike shorts made me think of Billy. Maybe I'd finally return one of his calls when I got back. I thought the fresh air in Costa Rica might be helping my head clear. I mean, why couldn't we find a way to stay in each other's lives?

Cynthia started holding up one flesh-colored thing after another. "The Slim Cognito Shaping Cami . . . the Power Panty . . . the Hide-and-Sleek Slip-Suit . . . each one more genius than the one before. They're just so totally brilliant I just can't stop buying them."

She plopped down on the bed again. "It could have been me," she said.

And then she started to cry.

I sighed. I pulled the door shut and put the empty suitcase on the floor. I sat down on the bed next to Cynthia, just close enough to pat her on the back while she sobbed.

Eventually I handed her a tissue. I hoped the heavy tissue use in our group wasn't negatively impacting Costa Rica's green rating.

"If only I'd listened to myself," Cynthia said when she finished blowing her nose. "I could have plummeted to the top of the fashion world."

"So this is about Spanx?"

Cynthia stretched her bangs back into place with the hand not holding the tissue. "No, it's about *me*. I don't know what I'm supposed to *do*. I mean, I have a head filled with ideas, but I can't tell the difference between the good ones and the bad ones until it's too late, so I just let them all drain right out."

I shook my head to dislodge a cartoon image of Cynthia's Swiss cheese brain leaking ideas. "But you have your work," I said. "You're an interior designer."

Cynthia took a raggedy breath. "Not anymore. My one lousy client won't be needing my services any longer. I think she misses her sink. But, I mean, farmer's sinks are so last year."

I flashed back to the night Seth installed that sink. I relived our first kiss in seven years, my back pressed up against the sink's white ceramic ruffles.

I'd managed to almost forget about Cynthia until she spoke. "Do you think I could do what you do? I mean, no way am I wearing one of those headphones, but if we can find something nice in Bluetooth, I think I could work with it."

Great, now I'd not only be taking Cynthia's kids off the bus, but I'd also be covering her phone shift while she finished her tennis lesson. I took a deep breath and tried to conjure up the most generous part of myself. "Talk to Joni," was the best I could do.

"Oh, thank you," Cynthia said. "I'll tell her you suggested it." Cynthia held her used tissue out to me. I almost took it, then caught myself and pointed at the wastebasket on my way out the door.

Walking slowly to give my Cynthia headache a chance to dissipate, I wound my way along the path that led to the hotel office, which also housed the computer room and a gift shop.

Tamarindo felt like the ultimate laid-back beach town, and our hotel was actually a collection of little thatched-roof bungalows flanking a free-form swimming pool and an open-air restaurant and bar. We were surrounded by lush, tropical growth and colorful gardens. An iguana dozed in the sun just off the path, and I was pretty sure I could hear howler monkeys chattering up in the trees overhead.

Best of all, the hotel was right across the street from the beach. I breathed in the sharp salt air. It was hard not to think about how much Anastasia would love it here. And I also couldn't help thinking how romantic it would be to come back again one day with a man. I knew Joni was right that it wasn't about the guy. But in all these years I'd certainly proven I could make it on my own. What would be so wrong about having a little companionship?

I could actually imagine a man in my life, as long as I kept the image blurry and faceless. The moment I tried to plug either Seth or Billy into the equation, anxiety grabbed my chest, as if it were choking off the blood flow to my heart.

I stopped to watch a pair of toucans up in a tree, looking like male and female Toucan Sams from the Froot Loops box come to life. Wait, why was I making this so complicated? Anastasia loved Seth. Life would be so gloriously simple if I could work things out with him, too. Birthday parties, school plays, graduations, even Anastasia's wedding one distant day. Simple. Simple. Simple.

So what if Seth was going to Japan on business? Was I sabotaging my chance for a normal life because I somehow didn't think I deserved one? Could the answer be as easy as a second try with Seth?

36

"CALL ME ISMAEL," OUR SURF INSTRUCTOR SAID BY WAY of introduction.

Everybody laughed, including the instructor. He was adorable, with shiny black hair and a chocolate, salt-licked body. "I think I've met him before," Cynthia said. "That sounds so familiar."

"*Moby Dick*," I whispered.

"You *slept* with him?" she whispered back.

Everybody cracked up.

"It's the first line of the book," one of the sorority sisters whispered. "Ismael was the narrator. Though, actually, I think it might have been *Ishmael*."

"That sucker ruined my junior year of high school," another sister said. "What was it supposed to be about anyway?"

"The human struggle for meaning, happiness, and salvation," the recently divorced woman named Janice said.

"Who knew?" Linda said. She was the woman who'd told us the bird story in San José. "And I thought it was just a guy book about whaling."

"I guess I should have actually read it instead of buying the CliffsNotes," Janice said. "Maybe it would have prepared me for the struggle for meaning, happiness and salvation in my former marriage."

Ismael walked away and came back carrying a long, beat-up surfboard. "I feel truly blessed for my country and all the beauty it has to offer," he said. "Surfing benefits your mind and body in the most positive way, stoked with more confidence in yourself and newfound energy."

We circled around him. He demonstrated a pop-up, essentially catching an imaginary wave and going from a paddling position, to lying on top of the board, to squatting, to standing on the board.

We watched, mesmerized by the muscles rippling across his back.

"Now again, but slowly," Ismael said.

The lawyer sighed.

Ismael lowered himself to the board. "The first part is much alike as a push-up with your arms. But with one flow, you must snap up to a crouch positioning as quickly as you can."

Too soon, we had to stop watching Ismael and attempt our own pop-ups. We chose beginner surfboards, which were short and soft, from the rack. I picked a white one with a vertical border of pink hibiscus along each side. Anastasia would have loved it. I couldn't wait to come back to Costa Rica with her. Maybe Seth would come, too. It might even be a second honeymoon.

Seth's and my first honeymoon was a three-night trip to a bed-and-breakfast in Bar Harbor, Maine. It was all we could afford, but we'd traveled so much already and Bar Harbor was breathtakingly beautiful, so we didn't mind. Our room was cramped with antiques and a canopy bed. It was like being caught in a time warp, so we called each other *my lord* and *my lady* while we lingered over breakfast in the dusty gingham and lace dining room. We meandered through Acadia National Park along Park Loop Road, pulling off to the side of the road to take in the staggering views or to explore a stretch of rocky beach. Or just to kiss. We walked the carriage roads and took pictures of the stone bridges. We splurged on lobster quiche for lunch, steamed lobster for dinner.

"I'll love you forever," Seth had said as we made love in our creaky canopy bed on our last morning there. "No matter what."

Maybe I'd love Seth forever, no matter what, too.

I brushed some Costa Rican sand from my hands and attempted another pop-up.

"Practice makes perfect, guys," Ismael said. I knew he was talking about pop-ups, but I thought there might be a message for Seth and me, too.

By the time Ismael moved on to teaching us how to add a half-twist to our pop-up, so that our feet and body were facing out away from the board, I was ready for a nap.

Instead we hit the water for some paddling practice. I did okay, but of course Cynthia was brilliant at it, getting all show-offy in her teeny bikini as she practiced her pop-ups in the water, even though Ismael hadn't told us we were ready yet.

"Enough of this lesson," Ismael finally yelled. I couldn't have said it better myself. I dragged my tired body out of the water and returned my sandy surfboard to the rack.

Cynthia was still going at it, so I walked back to our bungalow alone. I peeled off my new black suit and rinsed it carefully, in case it had to last me for the next decade or so. I took a quick shower and changed into shorts and a T-shirt.

I headed down to the office to check my e-mail. I bought a bottle of water from the ancient vending machine, then sat down at the single computer in the alcove across from the main desk. I took a sip and clicked on the Internet icon. While I waited for it to upload, I put one elbow on the old metal desk and rested my chin on the heel of my hand.

I closed my eyes and wished for an e-mail from Anastasia. I knew she was fine, but I missed her. I pictured her sitting on the couch with Seth last night, like two peas in a pod, watching TV. Family was the most important thing, and mine was at home, waiting for me.

I typed in the Web address for my e-mail, then entered my password.

The message I'd wished for was waiting for me in the inbox. I smiled and double clicked.

Hey Mom
I got a 100 on my spelling test and then we made
Japanese tempoora for dinner. Me and Cammy think
your prettier than Dads friend Ileen. Miss u.
Love
Me

I fumbled in my shoulder bag for my cell phone as I pushed the office door open.

I chose a random path and half ran, half walked, until I lost myself in the tropical growth. I leaned up against a palm tree, struggling to catch my breath. The howler monkeys overhead were louder now, screaming away as if they were talking about me. *Loser*, I was pretty sure they were saying. *What were you thinking?*

The sound of the waves crashing across the street merged with the rage pounding in my ears.

Eventually, I unearthed my phone. My hands were shaking, but I managed to find Seth's cell number in my address book. I pushed the Call button.

He answered on the second ring. "Hey. Everything okay?"

Just in case Seth had a sister I'd forgotten about, I said, "Who the hell is Eileen?"

"Oh," he said.

I waited.

"Just a friend. How's the trip going?"

I closed my eyes.

"Now I remember you," I said.

"What?" he said.

"Now I remember you," I said again. And then I hung up.

The monkeys screeched above me.

I looked up. "Thank you," I said. "You're absolutely right."

I pushed Redial.

"Jill?" Seth said halfway through the first ring.

"Good guess," I said. "Is she still in my house?"

"Of course not."

"Is Eileen the woman you lived with in Africa?" I asked.

"What?"

"You heard me."

"It's not what you think. She was in the area on business, and she just wanted to meet . . . to say hello. I mean, we were together for . . . we're just friends."

I drew a line in the hard-packed dirt of the path with the edge of my flip-flop.

"Seven years ago," I said, taking the time to enunciate each word, "you shouldn't have left us. Even if I wasn't hearing you about the kind of life you wanted us to have, you should have kept trying until I did. Because we were a family, and that's what families do. They stay together and they figure out a compromise. They don't sneak off in the middle of the night."

"I can't take that back," Seth said quietly. "It's water under the bridge."

For the second time today I pictured us on our honeymoon, walking hand in hand along the carriage paths and under the stone bridges, a lifetime of promises ahead of us.

"Sure it's water under the bridge, Seth, but who built that bridge? Who took off and left me standing on that bridge with a three-year-old? Broke and scared, with no one to turn to. Do you know what I went through? What our daughter went through? There's not enough water in the world to wash that away, Seth."

"Jill . . ."

"Joni was right. I was stuck, totally stuck. Glued to my little house, my tiny world, afraid to move. I don't know, maybe I thought if I stayed frozen in place, nothing else could happen to us. Or maybe I thought it might make it easier for you to find us, so we could all live happily ever after like we were supposed to the first time. God, what was I *thinking*?"

This phone call was going to cost me a fortune. I didn't care. I was sick and tired of worrying about money. I was sick and tired of being sick and tired.

I took a deep breath. "But I'm unstuck now, Seth. I am soooooo unstuck. I want a brand-new bigger life that's not about waiting for you to grow the fuck up. Don't you see? You're doing it again. We hit a bumpy patch and, suddenly, guess who's coming to dinner?"

"That's not fair, Jill."

"I agree," I said. "It's not fair that I'll never be able to really count on you when the going gets tough. It was a lot to forgive, but if we both gave it our all, I thought we had a shot. Instead, I leave for five minutes, and you're already cooking dinner with your old girlfriend and working on an escape plan. Or at least a backup plan."

"But—"

I gulped in some air. "I think a quick update of the rules is in order. One: any decision that impacts all three of us is first discussed by the two grown-ups in the family. Two: before we expose our daughter to anyone we have dated, are dating, or might possibly date, the two of us have an adult discussion about the best way to introduce said person into her life. Got that?"

"What are you really saying, Jill?"

The monkeys were quiet now. Just a few yards away I noticed a garden filled with an amazing array of orchids. It was practically right in front of my nose, and I hadn't even seen it.

"What I'm saying, Seth, is that I forgive you. And I let you go. I want us to be the best co-parents we can possibly be, but I'm ready to move on with my life. You should, too. Put Anastasia on the phone now, okay?"

37

CYNTHIA WAS SITTING ON HER BED, READING ELIN Hilderbrand's *The Castaways* and drinking a bottle of water.

"Joni just stopped by," she said, "to see if we want to take a belly dancing class with her."

"Damn right we do," I said. "Let's go."

At the door of the thatched-roof, open-air yoga hut that doubled as a belly dancing studio, I bought a chiffon hip scarf. It was bright turquoise, with rows and rows of gold coins that made a lovely tinkling sound. I deserved it, and I tied it around my hips without even a trace of guilt.

Cynthia chose a pale pink scarf with tiny silver coins, and Joni went right for one that was tie-dyed with sequins and coins sewn in a wave design.

A striking teacher with dark hair coiled on top of her head and exaggerated smoky eye makeup danced into the hut in full regalia: fringed and sequined bra, fitted hip belt, harem pants in the sheerest sea foam chiffon. She pressed a button on the CD player and smiled at us.

It seemed totally incongruous to hear Middle Eastern music playing in a hut in the middle of Costa Rica. It was soulful, exotic, and sexy as hell.

Our instructor never said a word. She brought us through a series of movements, isolating hips, pelvis, stomach, ribs, shoulders. She'd demonstrate, then we'd repeat. We made figure eights with our hips and shimmied our shoulders. We worked on traveling steps.

The dozen or so women in the hut were of every age, shape, and size. We moved with an energy that was sensual, feminine, life affirming. Nobody laughed or made self-deprecating comments about their bodies. Nobody said anything—not even Cynthia. It took our complete focus to follow the instructor's movements. I willed my rib cage to move without taking my abdomen with it, made my right shoulder jut forward while my left slid back, all with a focus that felt almost telekinetic.

The air was less humid here in Tamarindo than it had been in San José, but even with a ceiling fan, it wasn't much cooler inside than it was outside. Ten minutes in, we were all covered with sweat, but it only made our movements looser, more sinuous.

My head cleared and Seth slipped away. I actually felt him go, as if I'd been holding a helium-filled balloon closed with my hand so the air couldn't escape, and when I let go it sputtered and swirled as it became airborne, higher and higher until it was just a distant dot in the sky.

I felt lighter, too, as if I were transcending the weight that had been holding me down, holding me back. I didn't regret the years Seth and I had been together. We'd loved each other. We'd brought our amazing daughter into the world. What I regretted was giving him the last seven years of my life by not moving on.

No more. It was my time now.

I moved my hips to the music like I'd never moved them before. The coins on my scarf tinkled and clanked, clanked and tinkled, calling out to the universe that my future would be filled with abundance. I would always have enough. I would always be enough.

"Ohmigod, I think that was better than sex," Cynthia said when we finished.

Joni untied her hip scarf. "Let's not get carried away."

I walked past them and out the door of the hut, floating through the flowers and the sunshine.

"Hey, wait up," Joni yelled.

I stopped and bent down to get a closer look at a clump of orchids near the path. Each one was more perfect than the one before.

"What's the rush, girlfriend?" Cynthia said.

I looked up just in time to see one of my monkey friends swinging to the next tree. "I want to do it all. Yoga and zip gliding and butterfly watching. And I don't want to miss a single sunrise or sunset while we're here."

"Welcome back, honey," Joni said.

"DO YOU HAVE ANYTHING really hot I can borrow?" I asked.

"Sure," Cynthia said. She looked up from her magazine. "Just about everything."

"Black dress," I said. "Sexy. I never ever wear anything sexy. Not I'm-looking-for-a-man sexy, but I-like-who-I-am-and-I'm-not-afraid-to-show-it-to-the-world sexy."

Cynthia swung her legs over the edge of the bed. "Not a problem, girlfriend. It's about time you asked for some wardrobe help. I've been trying to send you a telepathetic message about that since we got here."

"Don't worry," I said. "I'm here for you, too." I opened our tiny refrigerator and grabbed another bottle of water. Between the surfing, the belly dancing, and the yoga class I'd managed to fit in after lunch, I'd gone through at least six so far today.

I handed one to Cynthia. "First of all," I said, "it's *telepathic*, not *telepathetic*. Now I think you're actually a very intelligent woman, and with a little bit of focus—"

Cynthia looked at me. She clunked her water bottle down on the bedside table. She flipped her magazine onto her bed like a Frisbee. "What is this, some new twist on *My Fair Lady*? You give me three new vocabulary words a day and I teach you how to dress like a ho? I said *telepathetic* because I meant *telepathetic*. It was a cross between telepathic and pathetic. It was a joke. Or do you need me to teach you how to recognize jokes?"

I looked at her. What a fascinating place the world was.

"Dress like a whore," I said. "Not ho."

Cynthia put her hands on her hips. "It's ho or no."

We stared each other down. I blinked first. "Fine," I said. "Dress me like a ho."

Cynthia reached into the tiny closet. "And just for your edification, *My Fair Lady* was based on George Bernard Shaw's *Pygmalion*."

"As was *Educating Rita*," I said. "Just for yours."

"*Pretty Woman*," she said.

"*Mighty Aphrodite*," I said.

"*She's All That, Mannequin, One Touch of Venus*," Cynthia said as fast as she could. She handed me a stretchy, strapless black dress.

"Is there another piece to that?" I asked. "I'm not sure this part would make it all the way around my wrist."

Cynthia opened one of the dresser drawers and handed me something flesh-colored. "Don't worry, the Hide and Seek Hi-Rise Body Smoother will shave inches off your life."

"I don't know," I said. I'd always dreamed of trying Spanx, just not in this hemisphere.

Cynthia handed me a black push-up bra. "Just wait. It'll be like you got a whole body transplant."

I carried everything into the tiny bathroom, peed for about ten minutes from all the water, and jumped into the shower. The bathroom walls, ceiling, and floor were tiled in rough ceramic, and the shower end was curtainless and identifiable only by the drain in the floor and the showerhead on the wall. As I looked up at the thatched ceiling while I shampooed my hair, a tiny lizard darted out of sight.

"Cute," I said out loud. "Just a little lizard. And not the least bit dangerous."

I finished my shower in record time. The lizard was probably just a government plant to keep tourists from wasting water.

By the time I finished drying myself off with a highly absorbent, naturally antibacterial, 100 percent organic unbleached bamboo bath towel, I was sweating again.

I picked up the Spanx body-smoothing contraption. *What the hell*, I thought.

"Cheesuz," Cynthia said when I came out. "Who knew you could look that good."

"Thanks," I said.

I stood in front of the mirror on the back of the door and spun around so I could get the full view. It was like I'd shrunk two sizes everywhere but my breasts, which seemed dangerously close to spilling out of both the strapless dress and the push-up bra.

"Wow," I said. I couldn't take my eyes off myself. "Okay, well, now that I know I can look like this, do you have anything a little more appropriate I can borrow for dinner?"

"*Abstemious, triskaidekaphobia,* and *supercalifragilisticexpialidocious*," Cynthia said.

"What?"

Cynthia smiled. "Those are my three vocabulary words for the day. Now you have to go out there and own that dress."

38

IT TOOK US A WHILE TO GET TO THE POOLSIDE RESTAU-
rant where we were meeting the GGG group for dinner, because Cynthia's strappy leather sandals were half a size too
small and impossible to walk in.

"This is ridiculous," I said as I wobbled along the path.
"I'm going back for my flip-flops."

"You can do it, girlfriend," Cynthia said. "After a while
you get used to the suffraging."

The outdoor restaurant was fairly crowded, so we stopped
at the edge of the patio to look for our group. A local band was
playing a wooden flute–heavy cover of Santana's "Black Magic
Woman." We rocked our hips to the jungly beat, and Cynthia
and I gave each other a couple of hip bumps. I yanked up the
black dress before I lost it.

In the center of the courtyard, three round tables had been
pulled together in the shape of a snowman. In the soft glow of
candles and palm trees strung with white lights, I could just
make out Joni sitting at the head table.

There was an empty table right in front of us, and a small
ceramic vase in the center held three pinkish purple orchids. I
reached for one and tucked it behind my ear. A stream of water
dribbled down the side of my neck, and I wiped it off with the
back of my hand.

"I can't believe I have to pee again already," I said. "I'll
meet you at the table."

Going to the bathroom in Spanx might not be that tricky under the best of circumstances, but in ninety-something-degree weather and tropical humidity it was going to be a challenge.

There was a little split in the crotch, but I wasn't sure if it was for ventilation or elimination, and somehow I wasn't feeling quite that adventurous.

Music and laughter floated into the tiny thatched-roof bathroom as I thought my options through. Okay, if I rolled the dress up from the bottom, and the Spanx down from the top, it should work, right?

I tottered on Cynthia's fancy sandals as I rolled her dress up under my armpits. Then I tottered some more as I peeled the stretchy fabric of the Hide and Seek Hi-Rise Body Smoother away from my hot, sweaty skin like a Band-Aid.

My torso was finally free, but the same elasticity that had taken inches off my midriff was now making it impossible for me to separate my knees more than a fraction of an inch. Slowly, I worked Cynthia's Spanx down around my ankles.

I sat on the toilet, my sweaty butt sticking to the biodegradable toilet seat cover. I took a deep breath and released my pent-up pee like a waterfall.

Just as I finished, I felt the hairy tickle of something on my left calf.

I looked down. Cynthia's black strapless dress was rolled up over her black push-up bra, my ankles were bound in Spanx, and a black zebra tarantula the size of a small country was crawling up my leg.

Leave it to me to die in a bathroom in Costa Rica just when I was ready to start living again. I only hoped Anastasia was strong enough to get through the loss. And that her heart was already filled with enough memories of me to last her a lifetime. Seth would take good care of her, at least I thought he would, and if he didn't, I'd find a way to come back and haunt him until he got on track again. Maybe I'd luck out, and the next world, if there was one, would turn out to be an endless whirl of belly dancing.

I forced my frozen body to move. Carefully, I wrapped a long sheet of toilet paper around my right hand like a bandage.

Centimeter by centimeter, I stood up, my heart pounding in my chest.

"One, two, three," I whispered quietly.

"One, two, three," I whispered again, because it didn't work the first time.

I flicked the tarantula across the room with my toilet-paper covered hand.

I yanked Cynthia's dress down. I tried to pull up the Spanx, but it was drenched in sweat and my hands were shaking. I unbuckled Cynthia's sandals as fast as I could, kicked them off, then stepped out of the Spanx.

I grabbed the sandals and threw the door open, waving the Spanx behind me in case the tarantula tried to follow.

Billy Sanders was standing right outside the door. I threw myself into his arms.

"What's wrong?" he said.

I pointed. "A tarantula. A black zebra tarantula. Do something."

He pulled the bathroom door shut. And then he kissed me.

"Wait a minute," I said when we finally finished. "What are you doing here?"

He held up one end of the Spanx. "Is there a story behind this?"

I yanked it away. "Don't change the subject."

Billy shrugged. "Well, since you weren't returning my phone calls, I stopped by your house. There were some kids playing in the front yard, so I asked them if you were home. A little boy said you went to Costco with his mother. Then a cute little girl in a pink headband said no you didn't—you were in Cost-Eureka. My dad had just mentioned he was heading over here for a meeting with Joni Robertson to discuss buying her out, so I put two and two together and tagged along with him."

"Your dad," I said.

"Yeah, he still insists on spearheading all new business decisions."

"I don't need you to buy Great Girlfriend Getaways," I said.

Billy squinted his raccoon eyes. "I didn't realize you were part owner."

"I'm not. What I mean is, I don't need to be rescued."

He reached over and opened the bathroom door.

"Don't!" I took a step away. "Can you just do something about that tarantula?"

"Sure. Shall I take out the trash, too, while I'm in there?"

"Never mind," I said. "I'll handle it."

I did the best I could to fit the Spanx into Cynthia's clutch bag while I walked quickly toward the restaurant area. A tray-carrying waiter appeared.

"Excuse me?" I said.

He stopped.

"There's a black zebra tarantula in the restroom," I said.

He shook his head. "What else is new. That's the only thing that sucks about living down here. It's friggin' gorgeous, but there's friggin' wildlife everywhere."

"Where are you from?" I asked.

"Boston," he said.

"Me, too," I said.

"Wherever we go, there we are." He shifted the tray on his shoulder. "This sucker's heavy. Have a good one."

I turned around, fully expecting to see Billy laughing, but he was gone.

I TOOK ANOTHER SIP of my caipirinha and glanced down casually to make sure my breasts were still ensconced in Cynthia's black dress.

"What a fascinating life you boys lead," Janice was saying. "Tell us some more about the bike biz."

I rolled my eyes.

"Yes, do tell," another woman said. "We'd love to hear all about it."

In our snowman configuration of three tables, Billy and his dad were seated on either side of Joni like eyes. I was way off on the left side of the stomach, between two women who were talking to each other through me. I leaned back in my chair to get out of the direct path of their words.

Joni had made a quick introduction when I seated myself at the table. Billy's father waved, and Billy gave me a quick wave, too. It was as if we'd never even met.

I took a small bite of mango salsa. I moved some black beans and rice around on my plate. I guess life was just like this: one jump forward and two big hops back. Things had been so clear a few hours ago. I was going to take control of my life, learn to soar on my own power.

Brightly dressed women chattered away to Billy and his dad like beautiful, exotic birds. Suddenly I felt boring and drab, the world's ugliest duckling. Billy hadn't even glanced my way. It was as if I were invisible.

I gazed up at the trees and thought I saw an anteater swing by, hanging by its tail. I knew Costa Rican anteaters were nocturnal and called *tamanduas*. They were also known as lesser anteaters.

I knew the feeling.

I checked my watch. As soon as I could excuse myself without being rude, I'd head back to the bungalow, get out of this ridiculous outfit, drop the stupid fantasies, and move on with my life.

But wait. This wasn't high school. Billy and I should talk things through. I'd explain what I'd just been through with Seth. How I was feeling about my life and how the time just wasn't quite right yet for a new relationship. He'd tell me he understood, that he'd wait for me. After all, wasn't he the one who said that life was a marathon and not a sprint?

At the head table, Billy yawned and put his dinner napkin on the table. He pushed his chair back.

I yawned, too. I picked up Cynthia's clutch and reached under the table for her sandals.

Janice yawned. The lawyer yawned. One of the women next to me yawned.

Billy stood up. "Long day," he said without looking in my direction. "Nice to meet you all."

"I'll help you find your bungalow," Janice said. "It gets confusing around here at night."

"Or I could," the lawyer said. "I think it's right next to mine."

"Thanks," Billy said. "I could use a good rescue."

39

I STARED UP AT THE CEILING OF MY BUNGALOW, WONDER-
ing if the rustle I was hearing was a cute little lizard or a black
zebra tarantula.

Because we were so close to the equator, the length of
days and nights didn't vary much with the season, and this
time of year, they were almost equal. Sunrise and sunset were
both sometime around five-thirty, which meant in another couple of minutes I could stop worrying about tarantulas and Billy,
and head down to the beach to watch the sunrise.

So what if I'd had a sleepless night. So what if half the
women on this trip wanted to walk Billy back to his bungalow.
I was moving on to a life of sunrises and sunsets, belly dancing
and yoga. I'd find a way to travel with Anastasia. Maybe I could
run a vacation camp for kids.

When I had the chance, when Billy wasn't being swarmed
by women, I'd talk to him. We'd smooth things over. Whether
or not his father ended up buying GGG, everything would be
fine. Sure, it might be a little awkward seeing him with another
woman, but I'd get over it. I just hoped it wasn't Janice. She was
a little bit abrasive. I mean, not that it was my business, but
with all the available women in the world, I didn't think he
should settle for someone like that.

I kicked my way out of the bamboo sheets and tiptoed into
the bathroom. I brushed my teeth quickly and splashed some
water on my face, on the lookout for tarantulas the whole time.

I tiptoed over to the closet, put on shorts and a T-shirt, and slid into my flip-flops.

Cynthia rolled over in her bed. *"Terpsichorean, munificence, polyglot."*

"Good job," I whispered. "Go back to sleep."

I felt Billy's presence on the beach before I even saw him. He was sitting cross-legged on the sand, gazing out at the water.

Before I had a chance to overthink it, I sat down beside him. "Hey," I said.

"Hey," he said.

The sand gave away to splashing waves, which blended into a skyful of intricate cloud formations. The colors were muted, all shades of gray.

A pencil line of orange sun appeared. We sat there silently, as if we were the only two people on earth, and watched the full sunrise show.

"Wow," I said finally. "I can't remember the last time I saw a sunrise."

"I can't remember the last time I missed one."

"Really?"

We both stared straight ahead. "Yeah," Billy said. "It centers me for the whole day. Whatever happens after watching that, I mean, how bad can it be?"

I took a deep, cleansing breath. "Seth didn't deserve me, and I finally let him go. I know it sounds crazy, but I feel like I'm actually alone for the first time. As attracted as I am to you, I'm not sure it's a good idea to jump into another relationship right away. I think I should work on my independence first, really fly with my own two wings. So as hard as it would be for me, I want you to know I'd completely understand if one of the women who walked you home last night . . ."

"Which one do you think I should pick?"

I whipped my head around.

Billy crossed his arms over his chest. "Janice was nice. But I think she's still got a few issues to work through. The lawyer's a possibility—never hurts to have a lawyer in the family. And somebody left a casserole on the front porch of our bungalow this morning, so I'll have to find out who that was and add her to the list. . . ."

I threw a handful of sand at him.

He grabbed my hand and pulled me into a cross between a hug and a headlock. "Couldn't we just relax and have our third date?" he said.

"NOT JUST A TARANTULA," I said.

"But a black zebra tarantula," Billy said.

"Okay, wise guy, maybe I have told the story a few times." I slid over a little so I could kiss him.

"So," he said when we came up for air. "Are you sure Joni's okay with you taking off for the day like this?"

I laughed. "Vianca and the surfing instructor had it all under control. And I have to say Joni couldn't get rid of me fast enough. I think she was just trying to get your dad all to herself."

Billy shook his head. "I wouldn't hold my breath. Not to downplay my catch factor, but that casserole on the front porch was probably for my dad. There's been a steady line of them at his door ever since my mother died."

"How long has it been?" I asked.

A little flash of sadness crossed his face. "Two years."

"Maybe he's just not ready," I said. "Anyway, if nothing else, Joni Robertson is a great friend to have."

Billy kissed me on the forehead, then glanced in the rear-view mirror. The taxi driver was focused on getting us over the bumpy roads in one piece. "I'm actually angling for them to move in together by tonight," he whispered. "That way you and I can have my bungalow."

"Sorry," I said, "but I already have a roommate, and I can't possibly desert her. Besides, what was that thing you said about life being a marathon and not a sprint?"

"A total pickup line," Billy said.

The taxi driver pulled over and dropped us off at the edge of the Avellanes beach parking lot, next to Lola's Bar and Restaurant. We made arrangements for him to pick us up later. We rented full-size surfboards.

"Wow," Billy said as we maneuvered the surfboards to get their weight evenly distributed between us. "Now this is a beach."

We walked past some crooked old trees and under a rustic little awning through a break in a wooden fence, then past a giant driftwood tree half buried in the sand. The turquoise water went on forever, and the frothy white wave breaks were long and smooth and encouraging.

"Stingray Pointers," I read out loud.

"No pun intended," Billy said.

"Shh," I said. "I'm trying to read."

STINGRAY POINTERS
Equipped with whip-like Tails that have serrated barbs, the stingray is Capable of covering the majority of its Flat body with sand. Only its eyes and tail are Left exposed. Shuffle your feet as You walk through the water—the stingrays will dart Away.

"I find the capitalization here quite fascinating," I said after I finished gulping.

"I'm glad my ex-wife didn't know about stingrays," Billy said. "We had enough issues with jellyfish."

"Siphonophores," I said. I dropped the canvas bag holding our towels and water bottles and kicked off my flip-flops.

"No pressure," Billy said. "If you feel like hanging around up here for a while, I'll just catch a few waves and come back."

"Don't be ridiculous," I said.

Surfing isn't much different from the rest of life: it's fun, but also a lot harder than it looks. I was dying to stay up on the sand practicing my pop-ups until they would have made even Ismael proud, but it was time to move forward.

Doing the stingray shuffle while carrying a big hunk of fiberglass attached to my ankle by a leash was like trying to pat my head and rub my stomach while floating a piano. But once I got in deep enough to lift my feet up, I did all right for myself.

In surfing, and maybe even in life, the trick is to use the calm between the waves to position yourself for the next one. I paddled in a prone position and rode a few waves in. Eventually I worked my way up to a sitting position, then graduated to kneeling until I tipped over. I was pre–pop-up, but I was on my way.

Meanwhile, Billy looked like he was on a tryout for a surfing movie. My paddling muscles were screaming, so I took a minute to watch him. A wave came out of nowhere, and the next thing I knew I was eating a mouthful of sand. I fought my way up to the surface and rested my head on my board.

Billy paddled his way over to me. "Come on, let's take a break."

I spit out another mouthful of sand. "I thought you were tougher than that."

We stingray-shuffled our way out of the water and carried our boards up. We dried off and spread out our beach towels.

Billy handed me a bottle of water. "Why don't you watch our stuff, and I'll grab us something from Lola's. Anything you don't like?"

I flopped down on my towel. "Yeah, stingrays. And tarantulas."

Billy bent down to get his sunglasses. "Don't you mean *black zebra* tarantulas?"

I reached for his arm. "Hey," I said.

He sat down beside me and swung an arm over my shoulders. "Hey."

I leaned into him. "I just wish we could freeze things right here. All by ourselves on this perfect day. No worries about what happens next, whether you'll call me once we get home."

Billy kissed me on the top of the head. "The issue, as I remember, was not me calling. It was you answering."

"Or whether our kids will like each other," I said. "Or whether you'll go off to Japan and decide to stay there with my old husband."

"Or whether you'll ever get a divorce from said old husband," Billy said.

"Not an issue. I told you, it's over. I'm calling a lawyer as soon as I get back."

"My wife and I used a great mediator, if you need a referral."

"God, you're so civilized. It's actually a little bit obnoxious. No offense."

"It was a lot more obnoxious when we weren't being civilized, believe me."

"And what about mixing our business and personal lives? I mean, if you buy out Joni, then I see only two choices. Either I'm jobless, or I'm sleeping with my boss."

"Do I get a vote on that one?"

I elbowed him. "Cute. It's just that this could all turn into one great big mess."

An enormous mud-covered, pinkish pig ambled across the beach and plopped down at our feet.

"I'm kind of over this nature thing," I said.

A surfer walking by bent down to scratch the pig on the head. "Hey, Lola," he said.

"Guess that's Lola," Billy said. "Maybe she's here to take our sandwich order."

"I've actually read about her," I said. "In one of the guide-books. She's pretty famous—I think she was even featured in a spread in *Gourmet* magazine once."

"Better than in a recipe," Billy said. "Life's messy. It just is. So we'll take our time and do it right. And remember it's a marathon and not a sprint."

The pig looked up.

"Such a pickup line," I said. "Don't ever fall for it."

40

"GREAT GIRLFRIEND GETAWAYS," CYNTHIA SAID. "FEISTY and fabulous mantasy escapes both close to home and all over the world. When was the last time you got together with *your* girlfriends?"

I managed to nudge my car door shut with my hips without losing either my cell phone or my Lunch Around the World supplies.

"It's man-free, not mantasy," I said.

"Oh, hey, girlfriend. It's a cross between *man* and *fantasy*. I've been trying it out, and I think it works. I'll bring it up to Joni at the next staff meeting."

"We don't have staff meetings. And don't you dare suggest starting them. Listen, can you get Anastasia off the bus for me? Billy's leaving for Japan today. . . ."

"Of course. Good plan—you should definitely spend some time with him to make up for all the bad things your husband is about to tell him about you."

"Thanks," I said. "You're a real confidence builder."

"I try. Oh, wait, a real call is coming through."

I dropped my cell into my shoulder bag and hiked the shopping bags up a little higher so they didn't slip out of my hands.

I made it to the kitchen counter without dropping a thing. I laid out the ingredients to make a *boca* feast fit for a *Tico*—tortillas, tamales, even plaintain chips.

Then I arranged the feathers and paint and brushes. I put the framed feather Anastasia had painted with hummingbirds, frogs, and flowers in the center for inspiration.

When I pulled out the hip scarves, the tinkling coins made one of the world's most pleasing sounds. Joni and Cynthia had loaned me theirs, too, so everybody would be able to take a turn. I'd stopped by the library on my way and had scored not one, but two belly dancing CDs, and I couldn't wait to check them out.

I was all set up and ready to go by the time my class arrived.

"Welcome back, honey," Ethel said. She was wearing a bright red sweat suit today with lipstick to match. "How was Costa Rica? Everything you dreamed it would be?"

"And more," I said.

T-Shirt Tom was the last to arrive. "I bet I know where we're going for lunch today-ay," he said. His shirt said SAVE THE MALES.

I pointed to my own T-Shirt.

"The direct translation of *pura vida* is 'pure life,'" I began, "but *pura vida* can also mean everything from 'you're good people' to 'the good life to you' or 'to life.' *Pura vida* may have originated in Costa Rica, but more than anything, it's a state of mind."

I smiled. "And I am so there."

PASSPORT
TO YOUR NEXT CHAPTER

CLAIRE COOK'S SEVEN 7SIMPLE STEPS

SELF. You can't have self-awareness, self-confidence, or any of those other good self words until you decide to like yourSELF, and who you really are.

SOUL SEARCHING. Sometimes it's just getting quiet enough to figure out what you really want; often it's digging up that buried dream you had before life got in the way.

SERENDIPITY. When you stay open to surprises, they often turn out to be even better than the things you planned. Throw your routine out the window and let spontaneity change your life.

SYNCHRONICITY. It's like that saying about luck being the place where preparation meets opportunity. Open your eyes and ears—then catch the next wave that's meant for you!

STRENGTH. Life is tough. Decide to be tougher. If Plan A doesn't work, the alphabet has 25 more letters (204 if you're in Japan!).

SISTERHOOD. Connect, network, smile. Build a structure of support, step by step. Do something nice for someone—remember, karma is a boomerang!

SATISFACTION. Of course you can get some (no matter what the Rolling Stones said). Call it satisfaction, fulfillment, gratification, but there's nothing like the feeling of setting a goal and achieving it. So make yours a good one!